Finding the Way Home

Marcie Shumway

A New Reality Publishing
South Paris, Maine

Finding the Way Home. First Edition.

Published by A New Reality Publishing, 54 High Street, South Paris, ME, 04281.

Visit our website, www.ANewRealityPublishing.com, for more information on other *Reality: It's All In Your Mind*™ materials and to view the full line of our books and products.

ISBN 0-692-59479-5
ISBN13 978-0-692-59479-7

Table of Contents

Acknowledgements...5

About the Author 6

Chapter 1..7

Chapter 2..10

Chapter 3..14

Chapter 4..19

Chapter 5..25

Chapter 6..31

Chapter 7..36

Chapter 8..42

Chapter 9..48

Chapter 10..55

Chapter 11..60

Chapter 12..64

Chapter 13..69

Chapter 14..77

Chapter 15..85

Chapter 16..91

Chapter 17..97

Chapter 18..102

Finding the Way Home
Marcie Shumway

Chapter 19..107

Chapter 20..114

Chapter 21..120

Acknowledgements

I want to thank everyone that has helped me to finally bring my dream to a reality, this book. I couldn't have done any of it without my husband, my beloved editor Jennifer Harris, and my publishing company A New Reality Publishing and the owner Christopher Harris. The support and guidance you three have showered on me has kept me going.

A special thank you to Jessica Woodcock of Lost in Reverie Photography. Her amazing photo graces the cover. She has been a friend, mentor, and cheerleader. I could not ask for a better person to be there to give me a high five or to wipe my tears.

To the beautiful people that were captured on the cover, Jenny Poland and Alex Bishop, thank you so much for allowing us to use your love to emulate that of my characters. You were truly the perfect fit. A thank you also goes to Gary Stevens and Connie Verrier for letting us use your wonderful house for our pictures. It was exactly what we were looking for.

Lastly, I cannot say enough about my muses (you know who you are ladies!). You all read my story and pushed me to publish it before that was ever my intent. This story would not be possible for everyone to read without you.

About the Author

Marcie Shumway has been writing short stories for others to enjoy since she was in middle school. *Finding the Way Home* is the first book she has published. She is an avid reader that thrives on the many books of her favorite authors.

Marcie resides in a small town in Maine with her loving husband. The two share their home with their cat, Kyzer, and their dog, Dani. They also have two horses, Chance and Dee.

<u>Chapter 1</u>

I had just removed my bags from the carousel at the airport when I heard my name. I set them both down and turned to brace myself for the impact I knew was coming.

"Duncan, you are going to have to let go a little," I squeaked, "I can't breathe."

The big man stepped back and held me at arm's length for inspection. Duncan Conrad was as much an avid outdoorsman as they came. He was clad in a long sleeve button up shirt, jeans, work boots and a baseball cap. His skin was already starting to tan from hours in the sun this spring, and his blue eyes were flanked by crow's feet from years of squinting underneath his well-worn hat. His greying beard and hair were well trimmed, and his smile was contagious.

"You look good my girl," he said wrapping one arm around me and grabbing my bags with the other. "A little thin though, Skye."

I shook my head and laughed, something I hadn't done in months. He had seen me on a business trip six months before and I hadn't dropped or gained a pound since. Then again, he had always thought I was too thin, forever sneaking me sweets from the kitchen or putting extra on my plate before passing it to me at the dinner table.

Duncan was my best friend's father, and from the first day I had come home with Chad to ride the horses the family owned, he had taken me under his wing and treated me as one of their own. His wife Karen had been no different, especially when my mother had passed away and I had needed a place to stay. They had become my second family.

"Earth to Skye."

"Sorry," I told him noticing we had reached his truck. "In my own little world."

"Thinking about a certain ATV man?" Duncan questioned opening my door and gesturing for me to climb in.

I blushed deeply and looked away before jumping into the truck, as he placed my bags into the extended cab from the door behind his. The man he had been referring to was my other best friend and Chad's "other half" JJ. When I had met Chad it been the two of them practically connected at the hip, but somehow they had let me in and we had become the three musketeers doing everything together.

Just before I had left for college I had realized my feelings for JJ were not just those of a friendship sort. I had fallen in love with him, as much as an eighteen-year-old can be in love. Duncan had known from day one, and it had become our little secret.

"There is something you should know," he told me once we had left the airport parking lot and were on the interstate heading north. "Lisa is trying mighty hard to sink her claws into JJ. He's gone out with her a few times, but I think it has just been to get her off his back."

I felt my heart breaking again as I looked out the window at the passing scenery. Jonathan Jacob Hunter, or JJ for those who were close to him, was the perfect guy. He was good looking, caring, compassionate, hardworking.

I didn't know one person that didn't like him. Growing up all the teachers had liked him and all the girls had had crushes on him. For some reason though, neither him nor Chad had dated much.

A group of us had become close, Chad, JJ and I and three others. We had done everything together through high school, and Lisa Brown had been one of the group. Sometimes I wondered how she had even become part of our group. She was a bit standoffish and tended to hang out with the popular clique when she wasn't with us. Where we were more country and kept to ourselves, she was more city and like to dress up and be noticed. I couldn't exactly be upset with either of them if they ended up together. I had no claims to JJ. I smiled up at Duncan when I felt his hand squeeze my shoulder.

"I will be fine," I told him touching his hand with mine. "Whatever happens, happens. Everything will be alright as long as I have you guys."

Chapter 2

Two hours later we were bouncing along the back roads in Birch Wood, Maine. Duncan and Karen owned a campground, if that's what you wanted to call it. They had a main lodge that also served as their home and held a commercial grade kitchen and large great room for any campers that wanted to eat with them. Near the lodge was a barn that housed up to twenty horses, a large riding arena, an above ground pool, and bunkhouses for the seasonal workers. Just beyond the lodge, in the woods, were twenty spots for tents or campers depending on what people preferred and ten cabins. Each cabin was different and had its own name based on animals well known in the state.

I put the window down and let the cool May air hit my face as we turned onto the final road that would take us to Conrad's Cabins & Lodge. The snow had been gone for a few weeks by the looks and the grass was trying it's hardest to turn green. We pulled onto the camp road and I sat up straighter in my seat drinking it all in. Everything looked the same as it had six years ago with minimal upgrades. New coats of paint glistened here and there, and the riding ring had been freshly chain-dragged that morning. The pool wasn't open yet, but the furniture had been cleaned and put out around it, and on the grounds around the main lodge. Duncan kept driving past the lodge causing me to turn and look at him with my eyebrows raised.

"Oh, there is one little surprise," he told me with a smile playing on his lips.

I looked back to the road ahead and noticed he was taking me towards the cabins. We passed a few and kept going. We were heading towards the cabin I had always joked about wanting to stay in, The Otter. It was usually reserved for honeymoon couples as it was a one-bedroom set-up that was away from the others. It was beautiful and was one of the few that boasted a view of the river on the back deck.

"Really?" I asked excitedly gripping the door handle.

He smiled fully and pulled the truck to a stop in front of it. As soon as he did, Karen, Chad and their daughter Morgan all came out onto the front porch to greet us. I couldn't have been happier to see them. I jumped out of the truck, all prior nerves forgotten, and rushed to Karen to be hugged. Tears welled up in my eyes as soon as her arms closed around me. It was like hugging my own mother all over again.

When I was done balling my eyes out on Karen's shoulder I allowed myself to be hugged and fussed over by Morgan. I couldn't believe she would be graduating high school in a month. She had grown into a beautiful young woman with long brown hair and brown eyes like her mother. She was just a bubbly as ever and couldn't wait to work side-by-side with me for the summer. I soaked in her positive energy and couldn't wait to work with her either. Morgan's personality was a welcome one after the dry ones I had been working with for the past two years.

Lastly, I turned to Chad. He had bulked up a bit since I had seen him last, otherwise he was the same strong quiet man I had remembered. His dirty blond hair was shaved close to his head, under his baseball cap, and his blue eyes were still just as piercing as his father's. I wasn't sure what I would get as a welcome from him.

He had come to visit me in New York when I had graduated college, as none of the others had been able to get away. It had been just what I had needed, however we had had a fight just before he returned home. There didn't seem to be any hard feelings though when he pulled me in to give me a hug and a kiss on the cheek. I inhaled his familiar smell of aftershave and horses, and squeezed his middle for all I was worth.

After getting reacquainted we all went into the cabin. Karen had set up a late lunch/early dinner for everyone. We made Italians and dug into potato chips while catching up on the goings-on around town. We also discussed the work schedule, and what I would be doing.

It was midweek so I would be starting the following Monday. It gave me the rest of the week and the weekend to relax and settle back in. I would be doing the bookkeeping, billing, payroll and also helping out Chad with the horses and the campers. Many outside camps brought kids in for lessons and trail rides. The Conrad's also offered overnight horseback camping trips every other weekend for the kids. Morgan would be a counselor, but would also be helping me in the office when needed.

Suddenly exhaustion came over me. We had all moved out onto the deck and Karen and Duncan were enjoying their early evening coffees while we all chatted. I hadn't realized how much the trip had taken out of me until then. I could hardly keep my eyes open and Karen noticed my fight.

"Okay guys, we should get headed," she told them motioning them back into the cabin.

I followed them all back in, shutting and locking the sliding glass door and pulling the heavy drapes closed behind me. Duncan had carried my bags upstairs to the loft just before we started dinner, so after hugging everyone goodbye and locking up the front door behind them I headed up there to gather an over-sized shirt and shorts to put on after I showered. I felt gross from being on the plane and knew the warm water would relieve my tight muscles and help me sleep.

A half hour later I was climbing into the Queen size bed in clean clothes and semi-wet hair. I set my iPod Touch to play country music and sighed with contentment as I closed my eyes. I was finally home.

Chapter 3

CLINK!

I sat straight up in bed and listened to the sounds coming from downstairs.

CLINK!

There it was again. Plates and glasses being jostled. I laid back down and took a handful of deep breaths knowing I had locked the door the night before and that it had to be someone that had a key. The panic slowly eased and I looked at my iPod to see what time it was. Seven o'clock. Wow! Eleven hours of sleep. I guess my body needed it after the past few weeks of packing up my life, and moving it back home.

Slowly I made my way to my bags and grabbed a brush to run through my hair. I had figured Karen had left food in the cabin for the morning, but I hadn't expected her to make me breakfast. While I pulled my hair up into a messy bun I made my way down the stairs never once really looking up to see who was actually in the kitchen.

I stopped dead when I reached the final step and looked up. There making pancakes, blueberry pancakes to be exact, in the kitchen of the cabin was none other than JJ. His back was to me so I took the chance to take him in. His dark brown hair was a little shaggier on top than I remembered, however it was clean cut around his neck and a baseball cap sat on the counter near the refrigerator that I was sure was his. He sported a long sleeve button up shirt with green, white, and yellow pinstripes that was rolled up to his elbows showing muscular forearms and blue Carhartt carpenter jeans that hugged a lean muscular butt and thighs with well-worn work boots. My heart fluttered and tears instantly welled up in my eyes.

"About time you came down," he said turning to set two plates with pancakes and bacon on the table, "I thought I was going to have to bring it up to you."

I stood there speechless. Seeing his face hadn't helped the sudden speech impediment that I had acquired. His green eyes met mine and his smile widened. I brought my hand up to cover my mouth and to stifle the sob that escaped without my control.

"I hope those are happy tears," JJ murmured coming over and pulling me into his arms. I wrapped mine around his neck, and buried my face into his chest.

I tried to stop the tears, but they just kept flowing. I am not sure if they were because I was just so happy to see him, if it was because the best friend that I had needed so much in the past six years was finally in front of me, or if the trials and tribulations of the past two years had just finally caught up with me. JJ never let go or eased his hold on me. I could feel his breath on my hair and his hands soothingly on my back.

Slowly the crying stopped and I felt like I could step back and look into his face again. When I did he brought his hands up to cup my cheeks and wipe away the tears. I smiled wobbly until I saw the tick in his cheek. He tried hard to hide it by smiling back, yet I had seen it and I remembered my secret, and part of the real reason I had come back home.

I pulled away and made my way to the bathroom to splash cold water on my face. I cautiously looked up into the mirror and saw the faded bruises on my neck and cheek bones. They were more yellow/green then purple now and without the makeup I meticulously put on every day they could be seen. Unfortunately, they stood out against my pasty white skin like spots on a leopard. I shook my head and reached for the wall where the towel should have been hung up, only to have it handed to me by JJ who was leaning on the door casing watching me.

"Let's have some breakfast and you can tell me what those are about."

I dried my face and nodded, turning to follow him back into the kitchen. I had never been able to lie to him, not that I wanted to, and I had never been good at keeping things from him. I sat at one of the places that he had set at the table and started to eat. I guess I had been hungrier than I realized because I polished off four pancakes with bacon and a glass of orange juice before I noticed what I was doing.

I finally looked up and found JJ looking at me with a knowing smile, that never touched his eyes, plus that tick of controlled anger was still in his jaw. I wasn't worried that it was going to be unleashed on me. JJ was not that kind of man. I knew though that if the man that put those marks on me ever showed up here there would be trouble.

"When did it start?" he asked as I pushed my plate away and pulled back slightly from the table.

"Two years ago when Chad came to visit me for graduation."

"Jealousy?"

"That time, yes. He knew Chad was trying to convince me to come back home and he didn't like it."

"Steve?"

I nodded and flinched when he said his name. I suddenly felt restless so I got up and started cleaning up the breakfast dishes. As I was putting the last of the dishes in the dishwasher I felt him come up behind me. I inhaled and tensed, purely from habit. He put his hands on my shoulders and placed his chin on the top of my head. Despite the fact that we had only been friends, he had always been affectionate with me and right now I couldn't have been more grateful for that.

"Your secret is safe with me, but you know you are going to need to tell them."

"I know," I replied leaning back into him and his warmth.

I needed the strength he projected probably more than he knew. He gave me a quick squeeze before pulling away. I closed the dishwasher and turned to face him, leaning on the counter behind me. JJ grabbed his hat and settled it on his head.

"I hope you know I didn't intend to come here and upset you," he explained writing a number down on the pad by the refrigerator.

"I know that."

"I came because I have missed you and wanted to see my best friend," he said stepping towards the door.

"I missed you too."

"That being said. I wrote my number down, so use it. Text, call, whatever. Anytime. I have to head to work otherwise I would stay."

"Thank you for breakfast."

"You are very welcome. How 'bout dinner Saturday night? We can get the whole crew back together?"

"Sure," I nodded hesitantly.

Finding the Way Home
Marcie Shumway

I wasn't completely positive that I was ready to see everyone just yet, however I did know that seeing them all at once was better than running into them each one by one and having to explain the six year gap multiple times.

He pulled on the brim of his hat to say one final good-bye and was gone. I went back to the table and sat down heavily in the chair he had been sitting in. I put my forehead on the table and closed my eyes. That certainly was not how I had expected our first meeting to go, or my first morning back in Maine to go.

<u>Chapter 4</u>

I'm not sure how long I sat that way after JJ had left, but I figured it had been awhile when I startled myself awake. I shook my head to clear the cobwebs and immediately went upstairs for my cell phone. I sent a text to Karen asking her to gather the troops for supper. Now that my secret was out to one person, I knew I needed to tell all of them.

As I found clothes for the day in my suitcase and grabbed my toiletry bag my cell phone signaled a new message. It was Karen letting me know everyone was all set to meet at the main lodge at six and that I should invite JJ to come along as well. I chuckled to myself, of course, how else had he known where I was. I told her I would check with him and ran downstairs, arms loaded, to put his number in my phone. Once I had it saved I made my way to the bathroom, sending him a message thanking him again for breakfast and asking if he would come support me while I told the Conrad's that night at supper.

The warm water definitely helped relax me and helped me to clear my head. I knew that telling them was going to be difficult and there was no easy way to do it other than just coming out with it. After putting on clean clothes I looked at myself in the mirror. Of course the bruises were still there from this morning. I decided that I wasn't going to put on any make-up. It was just as easy to leave them exposed. Plus, this was my family, they needed to know all of it.

Brushing my hair, I made my way towards the kitchen to take stock of what was in the cupboards and the refrigerator. Karen and Duncan had made sure I had everything I could think of. I had all the pots, pans, plates, cups, and silverware I would need, along with at least a week's worth of groceries. I silently thanked them and looked at the clock only to realize it was lunch time. I had definitely napped on the table longer than I realized. While making myself a light salad, I knew there would be a lot on the dinner table tonight, my phone went off signaling a text message.

Meet you at the cabin at 5:45. Anything for you... :)

I felt my heart skip a beat. There was no doubt on my end that my feelings hadn't changed, however, until I worked through the rest of the abuse issues I wasn't going to get involved with anyone. It wasn't fair to ask anyone to take on my baggage.

Knowing I needed to keep myself busy until dinner, I ate my lunch quickly and proceeded to clean up around the cabin and unpack my things. Karen and Morgan had done most of the work the day before so it wasn't long before everything was done and I was pacing again. Finally, I pulled out the latest Linda Lael Miller book I had been reading and lost myself in the storyline. That was the only way I was going to get through the next couple of hours.

KNOCK! KNOCK!

I sat up quickly on the couch, disoriented and confused.

KNOCK! KNOCK!

I scrambled up and opened the door. JJ stood on the other side looking at me with a lopsided grin. I rubbed my eyes and ushered him in, looking at the clock as I shut the door behind him. 5:40.

"Sorry," I told him running my fingers through my hair and grabbing my book off the couch, "clearly my body thinks I need to sleep nonstop lately."

He shook his head resting his hand on my arm to stop my movements.

"Don't apologize," he said, "you are healing. Obviously you have had a lot going on."

I smiled back at him and ran upstairs to grab shoes, socks, and a sweatshirt. Making sure I had everything, I ran back downstairs to run a brush through my hair and to brush my teeth. Finishing those tasks, I took a second to look in the mirror one last time. I took a deep breath and let it out. At least the bruises weren't as bad as they had been weeks ago, I thought to myself running my fingers lightly across the marks on my neck.

"Everything will be okay, ya know."

I didn't flinch even though he had startled me. I looked over at him, and again took him in. He was in Carhartt Jeans and work boots, this time he had them matched with a long sleeve shirt sporting the logo and name from his father's ATV repair company, Hunter's Rig Repair. The dark green of the shirt had his eyes standing out even more from his lightly tanned face. His goatee was clean cut and his smile was reassuring.

"I know it will." I replied pulling on my sweatshirt and zipping it as I moved past him. "I just wasn't expecting everything to happen so quickly, I guess."

I sat down and pulled on my socks and well-worn cowboy boots. Taking one more deep breath I grabbed my cell phone and started towards the door with JJ directly behind me. We walked out to his truck silently. He reached past me to open the passenger door, and I smiled at him. I forgot how much of a gentleman he was, always opening doors for women. I climbed in and admired the lifted Dodge as he closed the door and walked around to the driver's side. It was clean and had a nice rumble when he started it up. Some things never changed. The boy still liked his toys.

When we pulled to a stop in front of the lodge I froze. JJ had come around and opened the door for me. I didn't budge from my place on the seat. I didn't think I could do it. His hand warm on my thigh broke me from my trance.

"I will be right here with you the whole time," he reassured me.

I nodded and finally slid down to the ground. JJ gripped my hand in his, intertwining our fingers and never letting go even as he shut the door to the truck. He led me around to the front door and opened it, only letting go of my hand to put his on the small of my back to usher me in. He shut the front door behind us and as he reached for my hand once more I heard voices in the kitchen. We slowly made our way there. Duncan was the first to see us and his face lit up when he saw us holding hands, yet it immediately dropped as did the glass in his hand as he looked at my face.

I flinched as the glass hit the floor and shattered. JJ instantly pulled me against his side and wrapped his arm around my shoulders. I hid my face in his chest, tears instantly filling my eyes. Karen turned around sharply with the sound and looked at us with confusion, as Chad came running from the dining room, which was the next room over.

"I'm... sorry... Skye." Duncan stuttered as he reached down to clean up the larger pieces on the floor.

"Duncan, whatever has come over you?" Karen asked bringing him over a small brush and dustpan to clean up the rest of the mess.

He nodded his head towards us. Chad stood looking at JJ with wide eyes, obviously unsure as to what was going on. Finally, I pulled away from JJ enough to look the three of them in the face. Karen gasped and put her hand over her mouth. Chad's jaw did just what JJ's had that morning, ticked, but he was careful to control the rest of this facial features. Without thinking he reached out for me and I left the safety of JJ's arms for his. He hugged me against him and kissed my forehead. Duncan comforted Karen while JJ finished cleaning up the glass, and we all took a moment to pull ourselves together. Suddenly Morgan popped her head in the room from the hallway that we had just entered.

"What's going on?" she asked.

I turned from Chad and looked at her. Her eyes and jaw went hard. There was no denying she was Chad's sister. She didn't say anything but walked to me and gently rubbed her hand across my cheek.

"I'm fine." I told her covering her hand with mine.

"Why don't we all go sit and we can talk about it over dinner," Karen piped up.

She had returned to the counter that she had been standing at when we had entered the room. Everyone turned to grab various plates and bowls of food and made their way towards the dining room. JJ cut me off before I could follow and cupped my face in his hands.

"If you need anything from me just say the word."

"Just sit next to me and hold my hand," I told him putting my free hand on his hip. "As long as I have that I will be fine."

He leaned down and kissed my forehead lightly before letting go and grabbing the last plate on the counter. Ushering me ahead of him we made our way into the dining room so I could fill everyone in on the last two years of my hell.

Chapter 5

Supper started as it always had in the Conrad house, with everyone checking in. We went around the table and each person talked about their day and what it had entailed. Due to my being absent for the past few years they each went into a little more detail, including JJ who filled me in on his taking over his dad's business and how things were going. It was nice and helped me to relax again. When it was my turn I told them about my friend Eric bringing the U-Haul with my belongings and that he would be visiting for a few days before he headed back to New York.

While conversation buzzed around the table I snuck peeks at everyone's faces. They all seemed to be taking it in stride and didn't seem overly fazed by the nights' earlier events, except JJ and Chad. Whenever either of them stopped talking I could see the tell-tale tick in their jaws, and JJ's left hand never left my right thigh unless he was reaching for a plate being passed. It made me smile inside, but I had a strong feeling when the night was over he wouldn't come near me for a while. At least that was what I had heard in counseling and from various other women that had been through similar experiences.

As the meal came to a close conversation became more sporadic, and the glances my way became more numerous. Karen and Duncan cleared away the dishes waving the rest of us off to the den to wait for them to finish cleaning up. Chad led the way with Morgan, JJ and I pulled up the rear. I felt her hand searching for mine as we made our way down the hallway and I let go of JJ's to grip hers tightly. I am not sure who was comforting who. When we walked into the room I inhaled deeply knowing it would smell like Duncan's cigars. This was the room he retreated to each night to unwind.

Chad remained standing while Morgan made herself comfortable on one end of the leather couch that was there. I curled up facing the middle of the loveseat that was perpendicular to the couch and was pleasantly surprised when JJ sat in the middle with his leg tight against mine. Had this been a different situation I would have basked in the warmth of this body against mine and the tingles it was causing. Instead I let it keep me calm knowing I had that added support. Chad poured himself, JJ, and his father double shots from the decanter on the small bar. He brought JJ's over to him just as Duncan and Karen entered the room hand in hand. Karen joined Morgan on the couch, the two huddling together for support, and Duncan sat in the only recliner in the room as Chad handed him his glass.

It was quiet, much too quiet, for minutes as everyone settled in. JJ sat his hand on my legs that were curled up almost on his left thigh and intertwined his fingers with mine when my hand rested on top of his. I let out the breath I had been holding and started my story.

"Things with Steve and I were great for the first year. I am not sure exactly what changed things or what triggered the abuse. He had never hit me or even yelled at me. Heck, we had never even fought. That all changed the night Chad and I had our fight. I came back to our apartment emotional and upset, obviously, and Steve asked what had happened. I explained to him that Chad

26

had asked me to come back to Maine and that we had ended up having words when I told him I wouldn't."

I paused as I said that, looking up at Chad who had worked his way over to the love seat and was now sitting on the arm on my side. He smiled sadly at me. It had been a horrible conversation with raised voices and crying. Both of us had said things that we hadn't meant and had let our emotions rule. I regretted it all now.

"Steve then decided it was time to pick a fight with me. Telling me that Chad was in love with me and that he just wanted to take me away from him and that I wasn't going anywhere. He only backhanded me that night, but gradually it got worse. After that night he never hit me where anyone would see. It was always on my arms, torso, or legs. Places I could easily hide with clothing. Eric was the only other person that knew. He had seen my bruises one day. He is actually the one that eventually helped me to leave Steve and get back to Maine."

I paused for a moment and took a breath. I looked around at my family. Morgan was holding Karen as they both cried silent tears, Chad had moved to the loveseat cushion on my other side sandwiching me between him and JJ, and Duncan was leaned forward in his recliner with his elbows resting on his knees looking at the ground. When I dared a glance up to JJ's face his eyes locked with mine and were filled with warmth. He squeezed my hand reassuringly.

"The last time was the worst. I had told him that I wanted to come back here. At least for a visit if nothing else. He lost it. He beat me and strangled me until I almost blacked out. He also......took advantage of me......."

Those last words sent Chad bolting up from his seat to pace the length of the room His hands tightening into fists, and releasing periodically as he went. Duncan stood up and poured another round from the decanter for the three men. JJ slowly untangled himself from me and got up to make his way to Duncan's side. I felt my heart break a little. I had known that his affection would be short lived once he had heard the whole story. Karen and Morgan came over to flank me on either side of the loveseat, each gripping one of my hands.

"When he left the apartment that night I packed a bag and called Eric. He took me to the hospital and when I was released I stayed with him until I flew here. He helped me to get into counseling and to file charges. He also helped me to pack up my stuff to move back here. Steve was arrested but almost immediately released. Unfortunately, his parents have money and a really good lawyer. I do have a restraining order though, so he cannot come within 100 feet of me."

Duncan had resumed his spot in his recliner and was now sitting back with one foot resting on the opposite knee, his cup balanced on his other knee. Chad still paced and JJ stood looking out one of the windows into the night. His back was rigid with controlled anger. I stood up and let go of both Karen and Morgan.

"I am strong and I have gotten through this relatively unscathed. I DO NOT want to be treated as a victim, or as being weak. I DO NOT want to be treated like an invalid, or like I can't handle things. I am working on not flinching all the time or moving away when someone is in my space and is upset. PLEASE don't treat me any different than you would have if this hadn't happened."

Duncan stood and came over to take me into his arms. I melted against him and felt the weight that I had been carrying alone for so long lift. He rubbed my back and kissed my head, much like he had done the day my mother had died. Karen soon joined our hug.

"I am very proud of you," Duncan told me stepping back enough to look me in the face. His blue eyes bright with unshed tears, "but it doesn't mean I am any less angry with him for what he did to you or at you for not calling us."

I had expected that. I had known that all three men would be upset that I hadn't called them to come rescue me. Some day they would figure out why I hadn't. As it was I knew that it would be hard for all of them not to run to New York and track Steve down to inflict some of their own damage. I smiled kissing both him and Karen before turning to Chad. He had finally stopped pacing, but I could see the pent up energy in him. I also knew part of what he was thinking.

"It wasn't your fault. Steve obviously had some issues. I found out after that happened that he had a high school girlfriend that he used to beat on as well. It wasn't just me, and you did not cause it."

I saw the tick in his jaw. I made my way to him and hugged him. He was slow to put his arms around me, but he finally did and held me tightly. He kissed my head just as his father had and ran his hands down my hair to hold my head, looking into my eyes. I smiled at him and placed my hands over his, squeezing. Morgan came up behind us and sealed me between them in a hug. I let out a chuckle and gave them both a squeeze.

Finding the Way Home
Marcie Shumway

JJ never said a word. No questions were asked from anyone. Once all the affection was over it was silently agreed that my confession had been enough for the night. We all made our way towards the front door. I gave everyone hugs and kisses good night and made my way to JJ's truck with him moving quietly behind me. He reached around me when I got to the passenger door and opened it for me. Once we were in and settled we made the two-minute drive to the cabin in silence. He pulled up in front and hopped out without turning off the engine. I sighed as he opened my door for me.

"I can make it inside myself," I told him putting my hand on his chest to keep him by his truck and quickly kissing his cheek. "Thank you for everything."

Before he could respond I turned and headed to the cabin. I unlocked the door, went inside, and closed and locked it behind me without ever looking back. I knew if I did I would turn around and seek comfort. Unfortunately, he wasn't ready for that and I wasn't sure I was ready for the rejection. I turned resting my forehead against the door and cried as I heard his truck finally pull away.

<u>Chapter 6</u>

The next couple of days were quiet, which was exactly what I needed after the big confession to my family. I spent a lot of the time napping and catching up on the many books that I had purchased and hadn't had the time to read. I couldn't remember the last time I had had a vacation. It was wonderful. It allowed me to do some processing of my feelings, and to decide just what I wanted out of the rest of my life. That hadn't really changed since I was in high school, which brought me a lot of comfort. I wanted a husband that loved me, children to spoil, a home that I felt safe in, and a job that made me happy. Hopefully it would all come sooner rather than later, and hopefully it would be with a man right here in Birch Wood.

The Conrad's periodically stopped to check in with me, reminding me why I had moved back. All four of them were caring and warm. Nothing had changed even though everything had. No more questions were asked about Steve, or our relationship. They just came to sit and visit, to talk about nothing and everything, and to help me re-find myself. JJ on the other hand was distant. I received a few text messages from him as we were all still getting together for dinner that Saturday so we could catch up, yet they were all short and straight to the point. I could only hope that things would eventually settle down.

Saturday night finally came around and to say I was nervous didn't even cover it. I changed my shirt and pants three times before settling on dark wash jeans, a navy ¾

31

sleeve V-neck sweater, and my black heeled dress boots. I heard Chad let himself in, so I ran the brush through my hair one last time and rechecked my make-up before sticking my lip gloss in my pocket and heading down.

A long low whistle greeted me as I made my way down the last few stairs. I laughed at Chad and felt the blush creep into my cheeks. No matter who it was, it was always nice to know that someone thought you looked good.

"Why thank you," I gushed slipping into my jacket that was laying across the back of the couch, "You don't look so bad yourself."

Now it was his turn to blush. Chad was a very good looking guy by any standards, but my feelings didn't go beyond friendship. His Carhartt pants hugged him in all the right places, and his long sleeve shirt was pushed up to reveal tanned muscled forearms. When my eyes made their way up to his face he was smiling a knowing smile that reached his eyes. I rolled mine and grabbed my purse before ushering him out the door.

"You nervous?" he asked as we settled into the truck to head towards our favorite restaurant, The Pit.

"Very. Not quite sure what to expect," I replied honestly as I ran my hand through my hair.

"Everything will be fine. The only thing you need to be aware of is Lisa."

"Your dad already warned me about her. I have no holds on JJ. He can do what he wants."

"Skye, he doesn't want her. You know that as well as I do."

I shrugged and looked out the window signally that I was done talking about it. The rest of the ride was quiet.

We pulled into the parking lot ten minutes later and I thought my lunch was going to come back up. We parked next to JJ's truck and I got out before Chad could come around to open the door for me.

"When you are ready to leave you just let me know," Chad whispered into my ear as we walked into the restaurant. I smiled up at him gratefully and followed our waitress to our table.

Everyone was already there when we arrived. Kyle, Sam (Samantha), JJ, and Lisa sat around the table chatting. Sam was the first to look up and notice our arrival. She hadn't changed much since high school. She was still curvy and her blue eyes lit up her face when she saw us. She immediately bolted from her chair and engulfed me in a bear hug. I held on just as tight and let a few tears slip down my cheeks. I missed her more than I had realized. Kyle, Sam's husband, was next in line to hug me and slowly Lisa made her way over. Once we had all said hello, the others went back to their seats and Chad and I found ours. The only two remained between JJ and Kyle. Chad sat next to Kyle and smiled at me as I sat next to JJ. Lisa was on his other side and I saw her shift her seat closer to him as I settled into mine.

The conversation was slow to start but once everyone had their appetizers and a drink in them it went smoother. Kyle and Sam updated me on their lives as dinner arrived and I listened aptly. They had gotten married right out of high school and seemed just as happy as they had then. Slight touches here and there could be seen between them and secret smiles, but there was one thing that didn't go unnoticed by me. There was a sadness to their eyes. I couldn't remember hearing from the

Conrad's about anything happening over the years. I figured it was something I would have to ask Sam about eventually.

"So, what about you Skye?" Lisa asked cutting into her meat and popping a piece into her mouth. Her shirt and jeans were so snug that I thought for sure she would pop out of one of them.

"What about me?" I asked avoiding her gaze.

"What happened to Steve? I thought you guys were going to get married?"

I felt the color drain from my face and I took a deep breath before I looked up. JJ's thigh immediately pushed against mine from one side and Chad's from the other in a sign of support. I took a long drink from my beer and noticed that Kyle and Sam were watching me as well as Lisa.

"Steve and I didn't work out. That was part of the reason I came home. I didn't have anything or anyone holding me there. My Masters in Business Administration was complete from out-of-state, which is what my mother wanted and I had done a long three and a half years at Ouellette and Son, P.A."

"I'm so sorry to hear that," she replied looking at me intently with a slight frown.

I shrugged my shoulders as I took a bite of my meal.

"It wasn't meant to be. It was time for a change and I was ready to come home anyway. This is where I belong."

Everyone smiled around me except her. I knew this would be a challenge. She wanted JJ and my coming back was putting a damper on her plans. I had watched her out of the corner of my eye all night and she kept leaning into JJ, only to have him shift more and more in my direction. She was blatant about it that was for sure. I sighed inwardly. I refused to fight over him. It just wasn't my style. I wanted him to be happy and if he wanted to be with her I wouldn't stand in the way. Not to mention, I was broken and who knew how long it was going to take before I was fixed.

The meal drew to a close and I had to admit it hadn't been as bad as I had thought. The conversation and the company was great, even with Lisa and her little quirks. Sam and I exchanged numbers and promised to keep in touch. We all walked out to the parking lot together. I hugged Sam and Kyle before they made their way to their vehicle and Lisa gave me a quick one right behind them. JJ touched the brim of his hat and nodded, but made no other move to come near me. The two of them walked closely to us and both headed to his truck. My heart leapt into my throat as I watched him open the passenger door for her to get in.

I felt Chad's hand on my back as he moved me towards the passenger door of his truck and my autopilot kicked in. I didn't remember getting into the truck, the ride home, or going into the cabin. It was all a blur. The only thing I remembered as I climbed into bed was feeling my heart break a thousand times over, and tears that just didn't seem to want to stop.

<u>Chapter 7</u>

I didn't allow myself much time to be upset about the whole JJ and Lisa thing. After all I was the one that kept telling everyone that I had no holds on him, and he could be with whoever he wanted to be with. I just had to work on believing that.

The following Monday I started in the office and things happened in a whirlwind. Juggling bookwork, cleaning, and working the extra horses that had come in from the dealer had us all working fifty hours a week or more. It was wonderful! There was no stress, just a sense of camaraderie and family. I worked full days and when I was done I was so tired I crashed almost immediately after walking through the door of my cabin. Before I knew it three weeks had flown by and campers would be arriving the following weekend to celebrate Memorial Day.

"Stupid computer," I muttered as the computer I was working on froze for the third time that morning.

Just as I was about to bang my fist on the desk a hand stuck a Doc's Donuts cup under my nose. The smell of the French Vanilla had me closing my eyes and moaning.

"Thank you!" I breathed. "You just kept me from killing the computer."

Karen chuckled. "Guess we need to pick up a new one before next week, huh?"

"Definitely wouldn't be a bad idea," I agreed, "preferably before the camper's start arriving so I have time to get everything transferred and set up."

"I appreciate all you have done," she told me settling into the other computer chair in the office.

"Not a problem. I am loving this. So much more enjoyable than working in the big city. I forgot how much I missed it."

"We are happy you decided to come back home. We've all missed you," Karen said sipping on her coffee, "including JJ."

I felt the sting and covered it by sipping on my own cup and not meeting her eyes.

"Have you heard from him?"

I shook my head. I didn't really want to talk about it, but I knew that Karen wasn't going to let up unless I did. She took her job as mom very seriously and only had our best interest in mind.

"Simple text messages. Nothing substantial," I told her. "I kind of expected it after the confession of everything with Steve and I."

She grunted and rolled her eyes. "He needs to grow up and get a pair."

I spit out my coffee and covered my mouth as I laughed. My eyes watered as I tried to fight it. I just couldn't and laughed for a couple of seconds before finally taking a couple of deep breaths and recovering enough to respond.

"He doesn't know how to act around me. I get it."

"It's not just you. According to Chad he has been missing their weekly poker games too. He was supposed to help him with the lawnmower and the ATVs, and we haven't seen him yet."

"What?! Chad didn't tell me that!" I exclaimed setting my coffee down on the desk with a thud.

Karen smiled and shrugged her shoulders. It wasn't a normal smile though; it was the smile of the cat that just caught the canary. Her news had me seething. How could he do that to the Conrad's? Avoiding me was one thing. They had nothing to do with what had happened to me.

I got up to pace the small office and noticed a truck pull in next to the barn. It was JJ's and it looked like he was here to meet with Chad. The two embraced and walked into the barn. I let out a little of the breath I had been holding and the anger eased a bit. At least he was finally there to do what he said he would. JJ was never one to go back on his word. I knew that I had knocked all of their world's off-kilter a bit with my admission, however, that was no reason for him not to keep a promise.

As I walked back to my chair my phone let out a chime. I picked it up and checked it only to find that I had a message from Eric saying that he and the U-Haul were pulling into the driveway.

"I have to go," I told Karen grabbing my coffee and my jacket all at once. "Eric is here!"

"Go! Take the rest of the day off and get unloaded. We will be down later to help."

I kissed her quickly on the cheek and all but ran out of the building. Just as I got out the front door the U-Haul pulled to a stop in front of the barn. I ran down setting my coffee on a fence post as I got to the vehicle. No sooner had he stepped out did I launch myself into his arms. Eric Palmer was built, tan, and any woman's dream, too bad he didn't swing that way.

"Hey beautiful," He murmured gripping me tightly. "I have missed you."

"I missed you too," I told him pulling away enough to look him in the eyes.

"Bruises are pretty much gone," he commented running his hands down my cheek and my neck.

"Finally."

Eric kissed me on the cheek and released me. I turned to grab my coffee and noticed we had an audience. Chad and JJ had come out of the barn to see what all the commotion was about. Chad wiped his hands on a rag and was headed towards us with JJ trailing behind.

"Hey man, good to see you again," Chad greeted as he reached for Eric's hand.

"Good to see you too," Eric responded shaking his hand heartily. "I am looking forward to getting in some vacation time."

"You deserve it from what we hear. Thanks for taking care of her."

Eric wrapped his arm around my shoulders and pulled me into his side.

"Any time. Sorry I didn't call you."

Chad shrugged and smiled. "She's here now and safe. That's all that matters."

JJ had remained silent during the whole exchange, but if looks could kill Eric would have been lying on the ground. His green eyes were dark with fury and I was flabbergasted. I didn't understand it.

"Umm...JJ this is Eric. My friend that I had told you all about. Eric this is JJ," I introduced awkwardly.

"Nice to meet you," Eric greeted, just as I expected him to, putting his hand out to shake JJ's.

JJ hesitated before sticking his hand out and shaking Eric's.

"We are going to head down to the cabin and unload. Karen said she would be down later on to help."

"Let me just finish with JJ here and I will be down," Chad told us giving JJ a funny look and ushering him back towards the barn.

"Wow!" Eric exclaimed.

"Yeah, not sure what that was about. Let's head down."

An hour later we were knee deep in boxes and the Conrad's had joined us to help. JJ had taken off after finishing on the lawnmower and ATVs with Chad. I wasn't surprised even though I was a little hurt. I had hoped he would stick around and get to know Eric. I shook my head as I carried another box up to the loft following Chad up the stairs.

"Sorry to keep you from working this afternoon."

"Eh. It's not a problem. Getting you settled in is more important anyway."

I hugged him and soaked up that warmth and comfort that was Chad. I couldn't have asked for a better brother figure in my life. I was more grateful for that now than I ever had been.

"I'm also sorry JJ has been avoiding you."

"He is dealing with some stuff and has been really busy. He canceled on us again tonight."

I pulled back from Chad and scowled. That was it. I wasn't going to let this go on any longer. JJ had pushed my last button. We made our way downstairs to find Eric and Morgan unpacking in the kitchen. I took one look at my friend and knew what I had to do.

"Hey Eric, how do you feel about poker?"

40

Finding the Way Home
Marcie Shumway

<u>Chapter 8</u>

I felt bad about sending Eric off with the guys for poker, but I needed to take care of something. I figured he would have more fun being out with them than he would sitting around in the cabin. He might have been looking forward to vacation yet he wasn't one to sit still for long. Eric had gladly agreed to fill JJ's slot and had taken off a half hour before me to eat with Chad and Kyle before the game. With him gone I showered and pulled on a pair of well-worn jeans and an old high school sweatshirt that I was pretty sure was JJ's. Not wasting any time, I pulled on my boots, grabbed my phone and the keys to the company truck I was borrowing.

I pulled into Hunter's Rig Repair and noticed lights on in the shop. The showroom was dark, as was the log cabin that sat back in the woods behind it, so I knew JJ was inside tinkering away on something. I got out of the truck and slipped around to the back door. I picked up the ashtray for the workers and found the key in the same place it had always been. I shook my head with a smile at the familiarity of it all and let myself into the back door that entered the storage room.

The radio in the shop was blaring the local country station so I knew JJ hadn't heard me come in. I made my way to the main bay and found him hunched over the workbench with his back to me. I looked around and noticed not much had changed. Girlie posters still covered the walls, some from his dad's time here, and tools were spread out everywhere. I pulled the bar stool out that sat beside the only workbench that was empty as it served as a mini desk.

I watched as JJ tinkered on whatever it was that he was working on and I could tell the exact moment he knew I was there. His demeanor changed instantly. His back immediately tensed and he wiped his hands on a rag before slowly turning around. His eyes were calm but the tick was back in his cheek, his features were taunt.

"What are you doing here? Shouldn't you be entertaining your boyfriend?"

"I could ask you the same question," I snapped back crossing my arms over my chest.

"You are the one that broke into my shop," he pointed out tossing his rag down and putting his hands on the workbench behind him.

"I didn't break in. I used the key."

He let his guard down for a minute and chuckled. "Guess I need to move that."

"What's going on with you, JJ? Why are you avoiding the Conrad's?"

"I have been busy. As you can see there is a lot to work on here."

I looked down at the machine that was torn apart. Getting up from my seat I walked around the four-wheeler and stopped when I found what I was looking for.

"Bullshit," I stated crossing my arms over my chest once again looking at him.

"Excuse me?"

"This is your machine. It has your initials on the back bumper."

He cursed under his breath and within seconds a wrench was being thrown across the room, thudding

43

loudly against the wall. Despite my past I didn't flinch. He obviously had some anger to get out and if throwing things made him feel better then so be it.

"Better?" I asked uncrossing my arms and setting my hands on my hips.

"No," JJ growled looking up at me.

"What will make it better?"

Before I had the question completely out I was up against the only bare wall of the shop and JJ was pushing his lips against mine. I wrapped my arms around his neck and dug my hands into his hair. His tongue ran the seam of my lips and I released the breath I didn't realize I had been holding to allow him access to my mouth. Our tongues dueled for control and I felt a moan escape me as he rubbed his hands down my hips and around to grip my ass and pull me tighter against him. His arousal was pushing against my belly and I rolled my hips against his and changed the angle of the kiss.

We went deeper and memories started to flood to my brain. Memories of him and I naked on a blanket in the woods. Before I lost all control I pulled away enough to lean my forehead against his and took a breath. He didn't pull away. He still held me in his arms. He moved his head from mine to nuzzle his face into my neck. I hugged him close and rubbed my hand up and down his neck to his hairline and back.

"Better now?" I whispered.

He laughed pulling away enough to put his hands on either side of my head to brace himself against the wall. I looked up into his eyes and noticed they had calmed as had the tick in his jaw. I ran my hand down his cheek and around the line of his jaw. He turned his head to kiss my palm leaving his hands where they were on the wall.

"I'm sorry," he finally spoke, "I didn't know how to act or what to do with what you told us."

"I understand, but why did you avoid the Conrad's?"

"I felt like I had let you all down. I should have known something was going on, I should have been there for you, not Eric."

"I didn't want you there. Any of you. Not because I didn't love you or trust you. I was embarrassed that I had let it get that far. Embarrassed that I had lost control of my life."

"But you allowed Eric to be there for you."

"Eric wasn't a threat to Steve. Not like you or Chad were. I wasn't worried about him getting hurt. I was scared beyond belief that if either of you had come charging in to save the day that you were going to get hurt."

"I can hold my own."

I ran my hands down his well-built arms and back up the front of his t-shirt feeling his abs and pecs rippling beneath my touch. He let out a hiss and his eyes closed as my hands came back up to wrap around his neck.

"I know you can. I couldn't stomach the thought of something happening to the man I love. The man I have always loved."

His green eyes popped open at my confession. This time when he kissed me it was tender, sweet and short. Short enough that I tried pulling him back to me. He shook his head and put some space between us.

"What about Eric?" He asked stepping back to lean against the four-wheeler he had been working on.

"What about him?" I asked in return, confused.

"You must have feelings for him."

"Of course. Aside from you and Chad he is one of my best friends. I love him, as a friend."

"Does he know that?"

"Yeah, I tell him all the time. Where are you going with this?"

"I saw the way you two greeted each other and the way he looked at you."

The puzzle pieces finally started to click and I burst out laughing. JJ didn't know. Tears streamed down my face as I worked on controlling my laughter. It wasn't the first time the mistake had been made. Eric and I had gotten that reaction all the time back in New York.

"JJ, Eric is gay."

His mouth dropped open. He opened and closed it a few times, looking much like the fish we used to catch in the river. As the information set in he started to blush and ran his hand down his face. He shook his head and smiled at me.

"Let's get out of here and go for a ride."

I didn't have to ask him what he meant. I knew. I followed him out of the shop, stepping out the back door ahead of him so he could lock up and hide the key I had used to get in. I followed him down the path to his house. It looked the same as it had when we were in high school. It was a beautiful log cabin with two dormers on the front and a farmer's porch. A two bay garage stood next to it. A Honda Foreman sat out front and he pointed to it as he headed for his truck to grab something. I hopped on the back and easily caught the Carhartt jacket he tossed to me. It wasn't too cold out, but being on the machine and riding would make it a little cooler. I pulled it on and inhaled a smell that was only JJ's.

He pulled a sweatshirt over the t-shirt he had on, and pulled on a fitted baseball cap backwards. My heart skipped a beat as he gave me a smile and climbed on in front of me. While he started up the wheeler I inched forward until our legs were snug against each other. I wrapped my arms around his waist as he put it in gear and headed for the trail that ran behind his house. JJ's left hand came down on top of mine. I intertwined my fingers with his as we putted down the trail and sighed into his back. We hadn't talked about "us" or anything that had happened, however there had been a shift in our relationship for the better and I was happy with that alone.

<u>Chapter 9</u>

I felt much better after my conversation with JJ, and obviously he did too as he started coming around the Conrad's again. He and Eric even took a couple four-wheeler rides out on the trails while Chad and I were working with the horses and preparing them for campers. Life was taking on a nice comforting hue. I could definitely get used to it, but at the same time I was a bit on edge waiting for the other shoe to drop.

I spent the better part of the last camper free day transferring files from the old computer onto the new one. Karen had brought me in lunch, so I didn't have to stop my keying and saving files. I wanted to make sure I had backed up everything possible and had duplicates should anything go wrong. Just as I was uploading the last file my phone chimed I had a text message. I picked it up to see who it was and was surprised when I saw that it was already six o'clock.

Girls night tomorrow?

It was Sam. I checked the schedule and saw that we only had two sets of campers coming in so my leaving for a few hours wouldn't hurt and Eric wasn't leaving for another couple of days. Plus, he could always go do something with the guys.

Sure. Lisa too? Where are we meeting and what time?

While I waited for her to return the message I completed my upload and finished organizing my QuickBooks file. I started to grab for a folder off to my right to enter some newer invoices when I caught a whiff of familiar cologne and noticed a body leaning against the door jam in my peripheral vision. I acted as though I didn't know he was there and kept on doing what I had been intending to do. JJ and I hadn't really talked so I wasn't sure how I was supposed to act around him. Were we friends, trying to date, what? I didn't want to jump into anything, did I?

My phone chimed and I used the distraction to put my back to JJ and read the message.

Lisa too. Bring Morgan. Dinner at Applebee's at 6:30. :)

Perfect. Can't wait!! :)

Just as I finished replying I felt weight on the back of my chair as I was being turned around. JJ placed his hands on the armrests on either side of me. That brought him extremely close to me and I had to catch myself from dragging his lips down to mine. Guess that answered that question. I did want to jump into something, but only if the other person was him.

"You're done for the night. We are having pizza and movie night at your cabin."

"We are?" I asked raising my eyebrow at him and smirking.

"We are. Chad, Morgan, and Eric are already there or on their way there anyway."

"Well, I can't until you get out of my way."

"Oh," he replied smiling, "I will but there is one more thing..."

His lips met mine in one of the sweetest kisses I had ever received. He never touched me with his hands. Just his lips, and it was over before I could even react.

49

When I opened my eyes he was stepping back with a soft content smile on his face and his hand was reaching for mine. I took it, and once I had grabbed my phone and my sweatshirt, I let him lead me out of the office and out for a night with the people I loved the most.

The next day was filled with last minute preparations for campers. We made sure the sites were ready and did final inspections on the cabins. Chad and I also did a final run-thru with the horses and made sure all the trails were clear and ready to go. I was glad for the distraction as it kept me from overthinking the night before.

We had all eaten supper and had curled up in various spots in the living room to watch an action movie the guys had picked out. Before the movie had ended I had found myself snuggled into JJ's side with one of his arms around me and the other hand holding one of mine. I still wasn't sure where we were headed. I knew though that we were going to have to talk before too long.

As I helped Chad brush the horses and settle them in for the night my phone chimed.

Enjoy your night out with the girls! Don't let Lisa scare you off! :)

I chuckled.

Can't get rid of me that easily. ;)

"Talking to your man?" Chad asked with a smirk as he leaned his crossed arms on the stall door of the gelding I was working on.

"He's not my man," I responded over my shoulder as I finished cleaning out one of his hooves.

When I looked over at him I noticed something on his left arm just below where his t-shirt had started to slide up his bicep. I stood and moved towards him. When I was directly in front of him I reached over to pull the shirt up a little so I could see what it was. It was a tattoo that covered a large section of his upper arm.

"When did you get that?" I asked, surprised because I had never seen it.

"Not long after you left," he replied with a shrug. "A friend wanted to go get one so I tagged along and ended up with this."

I chuckled as I moved his arm around to check it out in greater detail. It clearly was a meaningful piece, not just some ink. The tattoo was of a lone tree with an empty tree stand at sunset. Hanging from the tree stand was a red and black plaid cap. The same style and color cap Chad's grandfather used to wear. At the base of the tree, under a single rose, was his grandfather's initials and the dates of his life.

"That is so touching, Chad," I told him rubbing his arm gently. "He would be honored."

I had only had the opportunity to meet Chad's grandfather once. It was right after I had lost my mom and had moved in with the Conrad's. Wally had accepted me just as the others had. He had been a kind and warm man that had taken his commitment to family very seriously. Chad had been his only grandson and the two had been very close. Hunting season had been very special to Wally, and the two shared the love of bringing home meat for the family's freezer. When he had passed away in his sleep at eighty, Chad had been crushed. The tattoo was a fantastic tribute to him.

"Hey, you ready?" Morgan asked poking her head over the stall door next to her brother's.

"Oh crap! No, I still need at least a quick shower and change of clothes."

I looked back at my phone and saw that it was already close to six. I stepped out into the alley way around Chad and locked the stall door behind me. I grabbed my sweatshirt and followed her out to the four-wheeler she had waiting for me giving her brother a wave as we took off. She gave me a ride to my cabin and I made record time in taking a shower and getting ready. I locked the door behind me and made my way to the truck.

Morgan was waiting by the main lodge for me so I stopped and picked her up, and we headed to meet the girls. I was nervous how it would go with Lisa, without the boys as buffers. I told Morgan my concerns and she shook her head and told me I had nothing to worry about. While we drove I also filled her in on all of my confusion about the whole situation with JJ. I needed a girl's point of view and she probably knew him almost as well I did.

"Do what your heart tells you," was her response as I parked the truck in the Applebee's parking lot. I laughed shaking my head. Morgan had always loved fairy tales and was just as much of a romantic as I was. We made our way in and found Sam and Lisa already seated.

"Hey!" Sam greeted jumping up to hug both of us.

Her and Lisa were on one side of the booth, so Morgan and I made ourselves comfortable on the other side. The waitress quickly came by to grab a drink and appetizer order, and as soon as she stepped away from the table we started gabbing like old biddies.

Most of the conversation was about old classmates and how some people hadn't changed. I hadn't even realized how far along in the meal we were until I looked down and found that more than half of my dinner was gone along with the start of my second beer. I looked up at the girls and noticed everyone was smiling and enjoying themselves. I was so relieved. Then the conversation turned to JJ's business and the night took the turn I had been expecting.

"It is so great working side by side with JJ every day," Lisa gushed sipping on her glass of wine.

"You work with JJ?" I asked stunned that no one had told me.

"Yeah. I have been for the past five years. I do his books," she informed me with a smile.

"Huh."

"He and I have gotten real serious since you left," she continued setting her glass down and steepling her fingers underneath her chin. "I'm sorry if you thought that you were going to come home and pick up where you left off, all those years ago."

I coughed as I nearly choked on the beer I had been trying to swallow. My eyes quickly jumped to Sam's and she shook her head. I had thought that she was the only other person that had known what had happened between JJ and I the night before I had left for college. I felt jealousy rage up inside me, and I squelched it down the best I could. Morgan had tensed up next to me and I set my hand on hers on the seat and squeezed it.

"I wasn't aware you two were in a relationship," I said pushing my plate away from me and catching the waitress's eye.

"We are taking things slow."

The waitress quickly made her way to our table with our bills in her hand and that is when I recognized her. She had gone to school with us and had been friends with Lisa growing up. I couldn't believe it. I sighed and handed her a bill without even looking to see what the total was. I squeezed Sam's shoulder as I walked past her and made my way out the door without waiting to see if Morgan followed. All I wanted to do was go home and crawl into bed. I was confused, hurt, and jealous. JJ and I were definitely going to have a conversation and it was going to be sooner rather than later. I was not getting caught up in drama again. I wanted a happy life without complications and damn it I was going to get it.

<u>Chapter 10</u>

The next morning, I woke up just as worked up as I had gone to sleep. My dreams had been filled with JJ and Lisa leaving me restless and tired. I heard plates clinking downstairs and when I inhaled I could smell Eric cooking bacon and eggs. I rolled out of bed and quickly pulled on clean clothes for the day. I needed to vent and get some perspective, and Eric had always been a good sounding board. As I pulled my hair into a messy bun on top of my head and reached for my phone to head downstairs it vibrated signally a text message. I opened it and was surprised at what I found.

Dinner tonight? We need to talk.

Clearly JJ had caught wind about what had happened the night before at dinner. My hands shook as I got ready to message him back. My emotions were all over the place.

Give me a time and place and I will be there.

I knew that we had campers coming in, but if I got everything ready ahead of time I didn't see a problem with getting away for a couple of hours. I knew that Karen or Chad would cover for me. Pocketing my phone, I grabbed a sweatshirt, just in case, and made my way down the stairs.

Eric was just setting the table when I reached the bottom. I kissed him on the cheek as I made my way to the refrigerator to grab the juice, but froze when I went to close the door. His bags were sitting by the door. It was Friday of Memorial Weekend, and he had been planning on heading back Sunday when the traffic would be a little lighter.

"Did I miss something?" I asked setting the juice down with a thud on the table.

"I thought I would head out a little early," he told me sitting down in front of a plate and loading it up with food.

"Because??"

"I know you guys are going to be busy and I don't want to be in the way," he answered simply, digging into his breakfast.

"And you miss the city," I finished for him with a smile.

He smiled knowingly and we ate the rest of breakfast in silence. I completely understood where he was coming from. The only difference was that my homesickness had been the opposite. While I was in the city I had had a constant ache for the country, wide open fields and four-wheeler trails through the woods. I had disliked the constant go of the city, the sounds of traffic and the insistent lights.

"So, are you going to tell me how last night went? You came in and went upstairs in a pretty big huff."

I sat back, pushing my plate away. I took my time in answering him. I felt like a jealous school girl and I didn't like it. Just as I was about to answer him my phone went off. Eric raised his eyebrow, but he didn't say anything. I looked to see who the message was from.

Dinner at my house... 7 o'clock... I'm sorry

"JJ," I told him as I got comfortable. "Lisa informed me at dinner last night that she works for JJ, and that they are in a relationship."

Eric shook his head and chuckled, "and you believe her?"

"Honestly, I don't know what to believe. I came home hoping that after all this time he would still be single and that maybe I would be get my chance. I also came home with a hell of a lot of baggage."

"He loves you, sweetie. I can tell you that by the way he looked at me when I first met him, and the way he looks at you and talks about you. You will get through the baggage and I think he will help you with that no questions asked."

"And Lisa?"

"She is just a lost soul. From what Chad has said she has always felt like the odd woman out and has always been in love with JJ. Unfortunately for her, he has always been in love with you."

I sighed getting up and taking my plate to the sink. I set it down and texted JJ back telling him I would be there.

"I sure hope you are right, Eric."

"I know I am. Just make sure you name your first born after me," he joked smiling and picking up other plates from the table.

I laughed feeling a little lighter about the situation than I had. We made quick work of cleaning up from breakfast and we headed outside with Eric's luggage. We loaded it into the rental car that him and Chad had picked up the day before, and proceeded to drive up to the lodge.

"I'm going to miss you," I told him as we pulled to a stop and got out.

"Not more than I will miss you," he informed me as he put his arm around my shoulders and we made our way into the building.

Everyone was in the kitchen finishing up breakfast, so we joined them for a final cup of coffee. After a half hour of good-byes and chit-chat I walked Eric back out to his car. I couldn't help the tears that formed in my eyes as he opened the driver's side door and placed his to-go cup in the console filled with fresh coffee.

"You will keep me posted on Steve" I asked him again for the millionth time.

"I promised you, didn't I?" he asked wrapping me in his arms.

I nodded melting into him. I was going to miss him terribly, but I knew that country life was not for him as much as I knew city life was not for me. The one positive about his going back was that he could keep an eye on Steve, and let me know if he headed my direction.

"I love you. Drive careful and let me know when you get home," I told him pulling away and giving him a kiss on the cheek.

"Love you too. Always, and will do."

I watched as he pulled away, and then I headed back into the building so I could get some office work done before I had to check on the campsites and the cabins that would be filling up that afternoon. I caught Karen as she was leaving the office to run errands and asked if she was all set that night for me to scoot out for a couple of hours. She told me that she was and looked at me as though she wanted to ask me something, yet she didn't and for that I was grateful.

The day passed in a blur. Every possible scenario of what could take place that night between JJ and I had run through my head leaving my nerves jumbled. I wasn't sure what was going to happen and I tried telling myself I wouldn't fall right into his arms without talking first, however, I had never been real strong when it came to him. All he had to do was smile at me and I was putty.

I sighed as I changed my clothes for the third time that night. I had showered, dried my hair in waves, and put on a little blush and lip gloss. Now I couldn't find anything to wear. I knew we were just hanging out at his house, but I wanted to look cute and comfortable. Finally, I settled for light blue jeans, boots, and a light long sleeved shirt with the Conrad's logo on it. Looking at myself in the mirror I grinned. Despite my nerves I looked good. I had gained some healthy weight and muscle since I had been home, and the bruises were all but gone and covered with a nice tan from working outside so much. I was happy. No matter what happened with JJ, I was happy and had been for the first time in years.

<u>Chapter 11</u>

I sat in the truck taking deep breaths. I could do this. It was just dinner and conversation right? We were friends and nothing could change that. I wanted him to be happy and if it wasn't with me that was okay. Right?

Getting out of the truck and heading for the door I could hear the radio blasting 90s country and I could smell barbeque. I smiled walking in the front door without knocking. There was no way JJ would have heard me anyway as loud as the music was playing. Sammy Kershaw was singing about the queen of his double wide trailer as I reached the kitchen. The table was set and candles had been lit. A bowl of grilled vegetables was steaming next to a plate with baked potatoes and my guess was that JJ was grabbing the steaks off from the grill on the back deck.

I made my way to the refrigerator and pulled out two beers. I didn't see one open already so I could only assume that he hadn't had one yet. I was just pulling two frosted mugs from the freezer when he stepped back into the house shutting the sliding glass door behind him.

"Hey," he greeted setting the plate, with the steaks, on the table with the rest of the food.

"Hi," I greeted back, taking him in for a moment. He wore a smile that didn't quite reach his eyes and his hair had tunnels in it from his fingers carelessly being run through it. Obviously he was just as nervous as I was.

When he came over to grab napkins out of the cupboard, next to where I was leaning on the counter, I did something that surprised us both. I reached up and put my hands on his cheeks before leaning up to kiss him lightly on the lips. He didn't pull away but instead leaned in to deepen the kiss a bit without touching me. I opened my mouth when I felt his tongue searching the seam of my lips and met his with mine. He groaned before pulling away to rest his forehead against mine.

"I was worried you were never going to let me do that again."

I smiled without saying anything and gave him another brief kiss before grabbing the mugs and the beers and heading to the table. He followed me with the napkins and sat at the end of the table to my right. Our legs intertwined underneath the table and we started dishing out the food onto our plates like we had been doing it for years. We made small talk while we ate, only talking about his business, the Conrad's, and Eric's leaving. It was unwritten that we wouldn't discuss Lisa until after we were done. It was nice, peaceful and damn near perfect. I was content and my nerves had finally calmed down for the first time since the night before.

When dinner was over we did dishes together and refreshed our drinks before heading to the living room. I made myself comfortable on one end of the sofa, turning so that I was facing the center incase JJ wanted to sit beside me. Before making himself comfortable he turned the radio on and left the volume low. The familiar sounds of a CD I had burned for him before I left for college filled the room. My eyes met his and he smiled.

"You still have this?" I asked, tears building in my eyes as JJ sat down on the couch beside me turning to face me slightly.

"Why wouldn't I keep the CD that the girl I loved made for me?"

The tears started pouring down my face. It was all more than I could have ever hoped for after everything I had been through. However, there were still a few things we hadn't covered.

"Lisa," I whispered wiping the tears from my face with my sleeve.

"She was my means of trying to forget you," he told me taking a swallow of his beer and then taking one of my hands in one of his.

"When?"

"The night I found out about you and Steve. I got drunk with Chad at The Pit and she followed me home. I just wanted to forget and make the pain go away. Now, unfortunately, she has become obsessed with me and isn't getting the hint that there won't be anything else between us."

Tears started up again. I couldn't very well be mad at him. After all I had been in a relationship with another man on all levels including physical. It didn't mean it hurt any less. I felt JJ's thumb running along my knuckles and I smiled.

"Where does this leave us?" I asked finally looking into his beautiful green eyes.

"I would like to hope that we can pick up where we left off, before you went to college."

"I would like that more than anything," I told him," but I'm scared. I come with a lot of baggage and need to find closure with what happened with Steve."

"And I will be here for you through all of it. Just tell me what you need me to do. I have waited for you this long. I am a patient man."

Hearing those words had my heart soaring. He had uttered almost the same thing the night before I had left for school. Telling me that he would be here waiting when I decided to come home.

Memories of that night again flooded my brain. The party with everyone, the bonfire, and my admitting to him that I was scared to go to college without all of them, especially him. I had told him that night that I loved him, and that I was afraid of leaving without showing him how much. He had been my first that night. We had taken a blanket and had snuck off from the others. Not far behind his house we had found a small clearing in the woods and I had lost my innocence. It had not only solidified my feelings for him, but it had also made it hard for any other man to compete with him.

"I want to be with you, JJ," I admitted moving so that I straddled his lap and took his face in my hands, "but I can't guarantee it will be easy and I want to take things slow."

"We can take things as slow as you want. As long as I have you, that's all that matters."

I sighed and pressed my lips lightly to his. This was how it was supposed to be.

<u>Chapter 12</u>

The day of Morgan's graduation was the only rainy day we had seen all spring. I'm sure she was thinking it was a bad omen, but I took it as a cleansing and a new start. These hundred and fifty young adults were about to close one chapter of their lives and embark on a whole new one. Some of them would go off to colleges states away while others would go closer to home and a few would bypass school all together.

I couldn't stop looking at Morgan, the girl that I thought of as my little sister, as she flitted around the room trying to do her hair and make-up. She had her father's long legs to go with her mother's hair and eyes, as beautiful as she was at eighteen, she would be a knock-out by twenty-one. It was amazing how much she had grown yet stayed the same sweet person she had been as a child.

"Why are you so nervous?" I questioned making myself comfortable on her bed.

"This is the last time I will see some of these people," she reminded me as she put the final touches on her lip gloss and tucked the tube into her overnight bag.

"Trying to make a lasting impression?"

"With some," she muttered with a shrug.

I watched her for a minute as she put a change of clothes and her bathing suit into the bag. Those that chose to from the graduating class, along with multiple chaperones, would be spending the night at the local college. It was chem free and was a way to keep the new graduates from making poor decisions on their last night as high school students.

"Morgan, there is more to it than that. Talk to me," I told her patting the bed beside me.

She sat down with a huff and toyed with the bracelet dangling from her wrist. I knew she would eventually come out with it so I waited, finally putting my hand over hers to still her movements. She looked up at me with a faint smile.

"Do you remember Jason Lyons?"

"Yep, his parents own The Pit right?" I questioned as his face slowly came to mind.

"Yeah. Him and I have been hanging out lately. Just as friends, but he is leaving early for school because of football and I'm not ready to let him go," she admitted, unshed tears shining in her eyes.

I gathered her in my arms and rubbed her back to soothe her. My heart broke for her. I knew exactly how she felt. I had felt the same way about JJ when I had left for college. It had been months before I had finally ventured out of my shell enough to meet people when I had gotten to New York.

"Everything will work out the way it is supposed to," I told her pulling away and gently wiping the tears from her eyes. "Enjoy the time you still have with him and cherish those memories when he leaves."

She bounced up quickly when her mother knocked on the door letting us know it was time to go. I followed her out of the room, carrying her cap and gown for her, still in awe of how much she had grown up in the past six years. When I saw JJ waiting with Chad and Duncan my heart broke for her all over again. I could only hope she could reunite with Jason years down the road as I had with JJ.

When we pulled up to the school I remembered why I loved our small hometown so much, everyone knew everyone. Despite the heavy mist there were groups of people huddled together talking on the lawn outside the auditorium where the ceremony would be held. I recognized so many faces, including many from my graduating class and those before me. JJ found my hand and interlaced his fingers with mine as soon as we got out of the truck. I could already see the curious looks, but Duncan and Karen led us directly in to find our seats, and out of the weather before anyone could ask anything.

The graduation ceremony passed much quicker than I remembered. Maybe because I was so caught up in all the memories it brought back of my times with my group of friends. I looked at each of their faces surrounding me as we waited for Morgan and thanked my lucky stars, for the seemingly millionth time, that I had them all back in my life.

Morgan found us and a small chaos ensued as Karen ordered everyone around for the pictures she wanted. Twenty minutes later I saw Jason approach Morgan, placing a hand on her hip and leaning in to whisper in her ear. She leaned into him and immediately a smile graced her lips and her cheeks tinged a rosy shade of pink. I felt an arm wrap around my shoulders and squeeze. I looked up, surprised to see Sam.

"Does that remind you of someone you know or what?"

"I just hope she is as lucky as we are," I replied wrapping my arm around her waist and giving her a squeeze in return.

Jason had come to get Morgan because the students were starting to change and load the buses for project graduation. She said her good-byes and waved one last time before leaving hip-to-hip with her crush. This time as I watched her I felt a pair of arms wrap around me from behind along with a familiar tantalizing smell.

"Mini class reunion at my house like our graduation night," he breathed in my ear before kissing my cheek.

I sighed with contentment and followed him outside to the truck. Even though I knew people would ask all sorts of questions, some that I knew I didn't have the answers to, I was excited to see people and reminisce. I had fond memories of high school and of my last night in Maine before college. I knew I said I didn't want to rush, but I was more than ready to repeat that night.

It amazed me how many people showed up to mill around and visit at JJ's home garage. I bounced around from conversation to conversation. I got your typical 'what's been going on the past six years?', yet no one ever asked anything more in depth than that. I also never got any reactions like I had from Lisa that night at dinner, though I could feel her eyes burning holes into my back from across the room.

When someone complimented me on how good I looked and how happy I seemed, I realized I hadn't seen part of that cause in a while. I turned around and found him within arm's length in conversation with Chad, Kyle, and a few other men. I smiled softly at him and got a wink in return. As I returned to my conversation with Jess Wing, a woman that had graduated a few years ahead of me, she informed me that JJ also seemed much happier since I had come back to town. The comment warmed me.

"How are you holding up?" JJ whispered in my ear a couple hours later.

"Fantastic!" I exclaimed turning to wrap my arms around him. "I'm really glad someone suggested it."

"Good. I love to see that smile on your face and that relaxed air around you," he stated while kissing my forehead and wrapping his arms around me to return the hug.

Eventually things started to wind down and it was just our little crew left. We all helped JJ pickup and put everything back in place before we took off. Just as I was about to climb into Chad's truck I was grabbed from behind and turned so my back was against the extended cab door. I raised my eyebrow at JJ since we had just finished saying good-bye with a very deep, long kiss, and that's when I saw her. Lisa had somehow maneuvered Sam and Kyle into leaving her behind and she wanted JJ to bring her home.

I looked to Chad, however he had already taken things into his own hands and was ushering her towards the door JJ had just pulled me from. I kissed Chad lightly on the cheek in thank-you as we passed him on the way to JJ's truck. Shaking my head, I climbed in when he opened the door for me and sighed. I hope she finds someone to love...

Chapter 13

The summer camping season was officially under way. The holiday weekend came and went. The weather was beautiful with just enough rain showers to help everything green up and grow, yet not enough to keep the campers at bay. They came in droves. The Conrad's and I helped them settle in and soon had all lots and cabins full. Chad and I took them out on trail rides with the horses and on weekends Chad and JJ took them out on ATVs. It was only a matter of time before we set up one of the weekend overnight rides that the campers enjoyed so much.

Morgan and I had even facilitated a couple shopping trips to Fledgemont with the women, teenage girls, and kids. The small town boasted many well-known clothing and shoe stores, as well as various tourist shops the state was known for. It was just over an hour away, so it made for a perfect day trip.

JJ and I hadn't had much of a chance to have a real relationship as we were both very busy. After I spent the days helping with campers I would spend the evenings keeping up with the books. Meanwhile it was JJ's busy season. Everyone and their brother wanted their machines worked on to prepare them for the riding season, or mowing season depending on what they owned. We had spent a little time together on the weekends, but it was only long enough to watch a movie and cuddle. We hadn't had the time for a real date yet, not that I was complaining. I was just as happy to cuddle and watch movies rather than be out and about dealing with people we might know.

Finally, on a Wednesday morning in mid-June I found myself free. Bookwork was caught up and Chad and Morgan were out with some of the campers already. I looked at the schedule and found that my day was actually pretty quiet, so I decided to run to Doc's Donuts and grab a coffee to bring to JJ at work.

Smiling, I parked out front and walked in through the showroom rather than going around back. Will, an older gentleman that had worked for JJ's father, was covering the showroom and stood behind the counter. I set a box of a dozen donuts down in front of him and laughed when he rolled his eyes and sighed in delight.

"You sure you don't want to run away with me beautiful?" he teased reaching in to grab a jelly filled donut.

"Sorry, but it might break a certain boy's heart," I replied winking at him. "Where is he at?"

"He'll get over it," he replied wiping powder off his lips. "He's in his office."

I waved as I made my way to JJ's office, smiling once again because I hadn't run into Lisa, however, it was short lived. When I reached the doorway I saw her working on his computer and JJ was bent looking at the screen, over her shoulder. It was purely innocent and professional yet the green eyed monster reared its ugly head again almost before I could control it. He noticed me first and his face lit up when he saw me. My nerves instantly calmed and I held the ice coffee in my hand out towards him as he approached.

"My guardian angel!" he exclaimed taking it and pressing a kiss to my forehead.

"I found I had a quiet morning and figured you could use a pick-me-up."

"Definitely could. Books are being a pain and we have a shipment of parts that is running late. Not my day."

"Sorry," I told him putting my hand on his arm. At the same time I touched him, I heard Lisa behind him clearing her throat. JJ rolled his eyes at me with a grin and turned towards the noise.

"You have Kurt coming in ten minutes to pick up his machine. You might want to go make sure it is ready."

He turned back towards me and mouthed an "I'm sorry" while he scooted past me. He tapped my butt with his hand on his way by, and when I turned to look at him he winked and smiled. I rolled my eyes with a grin and was getting ready to turn and head back out through the showroom when Lisa called my name.

"You know you really shouldn't come here during the work day," she said getting up from behind the desk.

As she stood up I noticed that she had on the shortest skirt possible without showing anything inappropriate. It was accented with three inch heels and a very low cut top that left little to the imagination.

"Oh, and why is that?" I asked crossing my arms in front of my chest and leaning on the doorframe.

"You are a distraction and *our* business doesn't need that," she informed me crossing her own arms in front of her chest and tapping her toe on the floor.

I stood to my full height and was fuming. I didn't dare say anything in response so I turned and walked out. I didn't even stop to say good-bye to Will. I was too angry.

71

How dare her! I was a distraction? Did she look in the mirror this morning? *Their* business? More like JJ's business. I drove home on autopilot and I didn't even bother stopping back by the office on my way in. I knew if I stopped I wouldn't get any work accomplished.

Once I reached the cabin I sent a quick text to Karen telling her I was taking the rest of the day off. She didn't ask what happened just responded with an 'okay'. I proceeded to plug in my IPod and cranked up Miranda Lambert before grabbing some cleaning supplies and setting to work. I knew it was the only way I was going to burn off some of my frustration and jealousy before I took it out on anyone. I needed time to think and to process before I talked to JJ again.

I was in the bathroom a few hours later scrubbing to the point I thought I might go through the tile on the wall of the shower when something in the doorway caught my attention. I turned to find JJ leaning on the doorframe with a weary expression on his face.

"What do you want?" I snapped putting down the sponge I had been using and pulling the gloves off my hands with sharp movements.

"To find out what's up with you," he stated simply not moving.

"Your girlfriend is what's up with me!" I exclaimed stepping out of the tub and putting my hands on my hips.

"You're pissed at yourself?" he asked smirking.

"Lisa!" I growled narrowing my eyes at him and throwing the closest thing to me which happened to be a tube of toothpaste so it didn't make the satisfying thump I was hoping for, which only aggravated me further.

"Better?" he asked raising his eyebrows.

I knew what would make me feel better and before I could rationalize anything I all but launched myself at him. My arms went around his neck and my legs immediately latched around his waist. As my lips met his, JJ's hands cupped my ass to hold me up against him. The passion that I put into the kiss was met by him with no reservations. He shifted position and put my back up against the wall in the hallway outside of the bathroom, and used that leverage to run his hands up my sides to my breasts. The minute he cupped them through my shirt I pulled out of the kiss and arched against him. The growl this time came from him as his mouth latched onto my neck.

"Upstairs," I mumbled bringing his mouth back to mine.

The command had him pulling back slightly to search my eyes to make sure it was what I really wanted, considering that weeks before I had told him I wanted to move slow. I nodded and brought my mouth to his neck and nibbled as he carried me up the stairs slowly. I felt his erection pressing against my core through both of our jeans and I started to throb in anticipation. The minute he set me down on the bed I pulled away just enough to get my t-shirt off. When I settled my upper body back down and looked up I found JJ staring at me, desire burning in his eyes. I didn't want to think, I just wanted to feel.

"Off," I said tugging on the hem of his shirt.

He never questioned anything, just did what I asked. As he reached to grab the back of his shirt and pull it over his head I felt my libido kick into high gear. There was nothing like watching a good looking man take his shirt off that way. It was so sexy I felt my insides melt and my underwear had that telltale wetness. I immediately reached for him when he was done, and pulled him back to me. Our mouths locked once again as I ran my hands up his defined abs to his pecs and around to his back. His muscles bunched and relaxed under my fingertips while mine danced and tensed under his.

JJ pulled his mouth from mine and made a trail across my cheek, down my neck, and to my breasts that were still somehow encased in my bra. He expertly reached around and with two fingers unhooked it, quickly pulling it from me. He latched onto my nipple suckling deeply setting a fire right to my core. I arched up and stretched to grab the button on his pants.

"Now," I breathed struggling to unhook his pants as he continued his ministrations to my breast. "I need to feel you in me."

That was all he needed to hear. He pulled away and expertly shed his pants, boxers, socks, and boots. I took the time to rid myself of mine as well and was ready for him when he came back to me on the bed. I spread my legs to allow him complete access and he took me in one quick thrust. I almost came undone with the feel of him entering me, and let out a little squeak as my body adjusted to the intrusion. He was larger than I remembered, but it felt so right. JJ stopped moving and pulled back to look me in the eye questioning. I pulled his mouth to mine and kissed him long and deep, wrapping my legs around him and linking my ankles behind his back. He set the pace moving in and out quickly causing the friction to build. I matched my pace with his and pushed my breasts into his face. He took the invitation, latching onto my other nipple and suckling. It wasn't long before I felt myself on the brink of going over. My insides clenched onto his member, and I felt him harden more. He was just as close as I was. I reached for the extra pillow on the bed and JJ grabbed it from me to shove it under my ass to change the angle. It changed it enough that two thrusts later we were both coming with such ferocity that tears came to my eyes. I had never had an orgasm so powerful and so moving.

As we laid there, him squishing me with his weight, I nuzzled into his neck and revealed in the fact that it was him in my arms. I listened to his heart beat in time with mine and took in the smell that was only him. I ran my hands up and down his back and felt him start to harden inside me again. I chuckled as I felt him shift and his lips started running down my neck. I was just beginning to feel my core start to stir when he suddenly stopped and pulled back to look at me, his eyes wide.

"Shit," he muttered, pulling out and away from me suddenly.

"What?" I asked as he reached for his boxers and pulled them on.

I immediately grabbed for the sheet to cover myself and watched as he paced the end of the bed running his hands through his hair obviously distressed. I was quickly growing worried that he regretted what had just happened and tears started to run down my face uncontrollably. I pulled my knees up to my chest and buried my face in the sheet that was over them. I felt the bed dip under JJ's weight and his arms wrapped around me.

"I'm sorry," he whispered kissing my hair, "I should have been more careful."

"What?" I asked again picking my head up and looking at him.

"We didn't use a condom," he told me running his hands through my hair.

"That's what you were so upset about?" I asked starting to laugh.

"Yeah, what did you think was wrong?"

"I thought you were regretting it already."

"Hell no!" he exclaimed moving to run his hands down my back. "I have wanted to do that again for years! And plan on doing it again and again."

"I'm not on the pill yet, but I think at this point in my cycle that we're okay. If not, we will deal with whatever happens. I didn't exactly give you time to think about it."

"That's true, but I could I have stopped. I don't want you thinking that I normally sleep around or do anything like this."

I smiled at him and laid back down pulling the sheet aside and signaling for him to climb in bed with me. While he did I pulled a box of condoms from the bed stand and set them on top. He stripped off his boxers and reached for the box while he nuzzled my neck. Soaking up the affection I spread my legs and invited him back into the warmth of my body.

<u>Chapter 14</u>

"So, are you going to tell me what set you off earlier?" JJ asked as he flipped pancakes expertly on the griddle later that night.

I looked up from where I was setting the table and smiled softly at him. He stood at the counter clad in only his jeans. His feet were bare as was his chest, and his hair was tousled from my fingers running through it. I felt more relaxed and content than I could ever remember feeling and I knew if this was going to work that I had to be honest with him. As he finished with the pancakes and brought them to the table I told him what had happened, and what she had said.

His face got hard and his jaw ticked again. He kept shaking his head while I also told him about the night at the restaurant. I put a couple of pancakes on his plate and ran my hand across his cheek causing him to smile.

"I will talk to her tomorrow," he told me turning his head to kiss my palm.

"Thank you."

The next few weeks found me staying with JJ at his house each night. I would finish my work for the day and immediately head there to make him supper, for when he got out. A couple of times he beat me there and had everything ready when I got home. It was nice to start and end the day with him. A kiss each morning and conversation about our day each night. JJ had talked to Lisa, and she had backed off. According to him she had even started dressing more conservatively. All was quiet yet again. Almost too quiet.

The fourth of July dawned bright and clear. I was up making breakfast for JJ by five as I knew I had to be at the Conrad's by seven. We had an afternoon/overnight ride to take a majority of the campers on. Morgan and I would be riding horses with some, and Chad and JJ would be taking the others on the ATVs. There would be fireworks and tons of fun. I couldn't wait.

Bouncing around the kitchen I mixed the eggs and milk I was going to be using to make omelets and reached for my cup of tea. As I poured the mixture into the warm pan along with a handful of precooked bacon and veggies I sipped from my cup and grinned. While the eggs slowly warmed I looked around the kitchen and dining room and laughed. I had stuff everywhere. Not literally, just little things. My mugs sat on the counter drying with his, my salt and pepper shakers sat on the counter beside me, and my spare set of sneakers were on the floor by the French doors in the kitchen with his. I had moved in without even realizing it.

"I didn't say anything because I figured you would move your stuff back to the cabin."

"Do you want me to move my stuff back?"

"Of course not!" JJ exclaimed coming over to wrap me in his arms.

I breathed a sigh of relief against his chest then pulled away quickly when I realized that I had forgotten about the eggs.

"Want to move your stuff the rest of the way in?" he asked coming up and moving my hair away from my neck so he could plant a kiss on the nape.

I took my time answering him. I flipped the omelets and when I was satisfied that they were done I pulled them off the warm burner. JJ had started on the toast to keep himself busy and from bugging me for an answer. I took the plates with the eggs to the table and went back for my cup of tea and the single cup of coffee that I had set the Keurig for him. When we both had settled in at the table and started eating I finally came up with my answer.

"I want to say yes," I told him not looking up from my plate.

"How 'bout we do a trial run and you keep the cabin just in case you want to go back?" he recommended as he put his finger underneath my chin and brought it up so he could look me in the eye.

"Okay......I'm just worried about us taking this too fast."

"We can slow down if you want," he said as he looked down at his own plate.

I reached over and cupped his cheek in my hand. He closed his eyes and sighed. I was more scared of losing him than I was of moving in with him. As it was we spent every spare minute together and every night, though we hadn't had sex again. I was so happy with how things were going, but I couldn't shake this nagging feeling that things were just going too well.

"I don't want to slow down. I want to be with you."

"Good," he breathed looking up again, "because I love you and I don't want to let you go."

I pulled his face towards mine and kissed him slowly and sweetly. Despite my fears I wanted to move in with him. He made me feel safe, he made me happy, and I hoped he was my future.

When we got to the Conrad's the preparations were in full swing. The plan was to leave around noon and it was a three hour ride to the camping spot. We would spend the next few hours packing up hay and buckets for the horses, extra gas cans and toolboxes for the ATVs, and organizing which guests would ride with who. Kyle and Sam would even be going with us and would be driving two side-by-sides full of gear and supplies.

Once all the supplies were packed families started to wander towards the barn where we were getting ready. Morgan and I tacked up our horses first and then proceeded to help those that needed it. Some were seasoned riders while others had only ridden here at the lodge. Morgan was going to take those that wanted to move a little faster on the ride ahead and I would keep those content with the slower pace with me.

Chad and JJ had split the ATV riders as well. Chad would take those that wanted to go faster and JJ would take those that wanted to take in the scenery. They all had a different route from us, a longer route, as the horses moved slower as a general rule. Kyle and Sam would follow behind me and my riders in case there was a problem.

As we were doing final checks on saddles and helmets I felt strong arms circle my waist and a broad chest at my back. I smiled and squeezed my arms around his. Some of the teenage girls looked on crestfallen as JJ turned me and kissed me. I slapped him playfully and pushed him away so I could get back to my duties. He feigned hurt but winked at me, and at the pouting teenagers before making his way back to his machine.

Finding the Way Home
Marcie Shumway

Finally, everyone was mounted up and ready to go. We headed towards the trail and within ten minutes I was pulled into utter peace. Conversations behind me were only slight murmurs as everyone took in the beautiful landscape and the constant rhythm of the horse's feet hitting the ground was music to my ears. I let my body completely relax in the saddle and turned around to check on everyone else. They all seemed to be enjoying themselves and no one was in any sort of distress so I turned back around to concentrate on the trail ahead.

I was just sitting back after having leaned down to give Rusty's neck an affectionate scratch when I heard someone come up beside me. I snapped my head in the direction of the noise, concerned because none of the riders had alerted me that there was a problem. When I saw who it was I smiled in relief. It was Nana Cody. Or at least that's what she had told us to call her. Nana Cody, along with Nana Beal and Nana Alexander had come for a vacation at the lodge away from their husbands. They still needed girl time too they told us and they had been a blessing to be around.

"How are you doing Nana?" I asked as she pulled her horse up to walk alongside mine.

"This is just the most gorgeous ride dear," she gushed.

"It is one of my favorites."

"So, who was the handsome young man we saw you with before we left?" she questioned.

I chuckled. I saw no point in getting upset about people being nosey about my relationship status. Instead, I found it kind of sweet that these older ladies had taken an interest in my little-ole life.

81

"His name is JJ Hunter and he is my boyfriend."

It was the first time I had said that out loud. While Nana went on about young love and how she had found her husband when she was a teenager, I found myself drifting back to the day I had realized it wasn't just friendship for me with JJ.

"You do know you're supposed to stay on the horse?" JJ chuckled as he reined his horse to a stop where I sat on the trail.

The new camp horse I had been riding had decided that the squirrel on the rocks beside the trail was a big hairy beast and had unceremoniously dumped me before heading back to the lodge. Unfortunately, we were forty-five minutes out onto the trails. I wasn't hurt per se, but my pride had definitely taken a hit. I glared up at him and felt my cheeks get unusually warm.

"Sorry," he apologized. "Are you okay?"

"Yes," I mumbled getting up and brushing myself off. "I'm fine."

"Come on," he urged putting his hand out for mine. "We'll double back."

I easily pulled myself up behind him on the horse using the stirrup he had taken his foot out of for leverage. We had ridden like this dozens of times, including with Chad, however, this time it felt different. I felt unfamiliar tingles running through my body and all I wanted to do was hold him as close as he would let me. JJ had filled out a lot over the spring and his fifteen-year-old frame was covered in newly formed muscles from working out with Chad. Suddenly I realized what was going on. I was checking him out like I did the other boys at school, he was no longer just one of my best friends. I wrapped my arms around him to hold on as he nudged the horse to move forward. I kept my body from touching his other than my hands because I wasn't sure of this new development.

"You good?" he asked pulling my hands tighter around him and resting one of his over mine.

"Yep," I croaked letting my chest come in contact with his back.

Oh man, I was in trouble.

Shaking my head, I smiled. Little had I known. The nanas were all now riding up front with me and pulled me into a conversation about their "wilder" days. It was comforting to listen to them and hear their banter. They stayed with me until we neared the end of the ride and I was almost disappointed that it was over, until I caught sight of those on the ATVs. I couldn't wait to spend some time with my friends.

I got off my horse first, along with Morgan, and we proceeded to help the others untack and settle all the horses into the makeshift run-ins. The guests all wandered off, either to enjoy a dip in the river or to help set up for the evening meal that Chad and Kyle were preparing. Morgan and I worked in comfortable silence to hay and water all of the horses. When we finished I wanted to run a quick brush over Rusty to clean the trail dust off and thank him for the ride. While I was opening his gate I heard JJ laugh. I looked over and him and Kyle stood side by side with toddlers on their hips. My heart caught in my throat at the sight of it. He was a natural, so comfortable with the little boy that was playing with the gold chain hanging around JJ's neck. Then I looked over at Sam and all my happiness disappeared. Her face was so riddled in pain and sadness that my heart broke. Clearly something had happened to bring that about, however she had yet to confide in me. Hopefully she would feel like she could soon.

Chapter 15

His face was all I could see as he held my hands above my head and forced his tongue into my mouth. I bit down and turned my head fighting him with all I had. Steve used his knee to separate my legs and wedged his legs between mine. My legs quivered with the effort of trying to get around his. I twisted and turned keeping my face constantly moving so that he couldn't try to kiss me again. Suddenly my hands were free, but before I could try to fight him off his were around my neck. His brown eyes bore into mine as I struggled to breathe and his smile turned to a sneer as I started to pull at his fingers with my own.

"Baby, it's okay. It's me. JJ. I'm right here. I've got you."

My eyes popped open and I looked around me quickly. I was in JJ's bedroom at his house and he was holding me tightly in his arms. I closed my eyes and worked on steadying my heart and slowing down my breathing. JJ loosened his hold on me and rubbed one hand up and down my back while the other gripped my hand. I felt clammy and shaken. It had been months since I had had a nightmare. Once I had returned to Maine they had stopped, along with the panic attacks.

I slowly got up and made a trip to the bathroom to throw cold water on my face. When I looked at myself in the mirror I actually didn't look too bad. My eyes looked tired, but not wide, and there was a tinge of pink to my cheeks which always happened when I had a nightmare. Having JJ there had definitely helped it from developing any further, yet I knew what my subconscious was telling me. I wasn't ready for this to be a permanent move. I needed a few nights back at the cabin to get some perspective.

I made my way back to bed and found JJ waiting patiently for me. He didn't say anything, just pulled back the sheet and allowed me to settle into his arms. I laid my head against his chest and held onto him as tight as I could. I fell asleep listening to the comforting sound of his heart beating steady and strong in my ear.

The next morning, I was up before JJ. Rather than waiting for him to get up I grabbed some clothes, my cell phone, and my shoes and went out to my truck in my pajamas. It was early enough that I could sneak back to the cabin and clean up there for the day. It was a quiet day of office work for me, which I was grateful for because I needed time to think and paperwork always relaxed me.

After showering and dressing in clean comfortable clothes at the cabin I made my way over to the office knowing that it would be empty. I wasn't ready to run into anyone while my thoughts were so scattered and I couldn't stomach the thought of breakfast with the butterflies that had taken flight. I had been at work buried in paper for an hour when a Doc's Donuts iced coffee and breakfast sandwich magically appeared at my elbow. No questions were asked. Karen just left it and brushed a kiss over my forehead on her way back out. Obviously she had talked to JJ and knew I needed my space.

As I made my way back to the cabin that evening I felt a little better. The Conrad's had left me alone all day, and I had spent the day organizing, filing paperwork, creating invoices, paying bills, and entering work into the computer. It had been just what I needed. My phone had vibrated only once during the day with a text message from JJ reminding me that he loved me and that he was here for me no matter what. Another smile graced my lips as I entered the cabin. I was so lucky to have a man like him in my life, a man that just went along with the rollercoaster of my emotions. Hopefully a couple of days on my own again would help me put some things into perspective and decide what was best.

Karen had made sure that my refrigerator was well stocked once again and I silently made a mental note to thank her profusely the next morning. After a large plate of pasta salad, I took a pint of ice cream and made my way upstairs to settle in for the night. Sending a quick text to JJ I climbed into bed with my ice cream and the latest Nora Robert's book. It didn't take long before my eyes felt heavy. I took the ice cream back down to the freezer and went back up to continue reading. Soon I felt myself drifting off again.

Steve backhanded me and I went stumbling backwards, my back colliding hard with the wall behind me. I felt my breath catch like I had been punched in the stomach, and looked around for a means of escape. I was in JJ's house. He had found me. Panic began to encase me as he came towards me, a smile on his lips. Where was JJ? What had Steve done to him? He backhanded me once again, this time bringing me to my knees. That was when I saw him. JJ was laying on the floor in a pool of blood not moving. I let out a strangled cry and I was lifted to my feet again. Steve's hands immediately went to my throat, and with one final look towards JJ, I stopped fighting. It wasn't worth it any more.

I woke up struggling to breathe. I looked around wide eyed and I was back in my room at the cabin with the light on the bedside table still on. I fumbled for my phone in a panic. I needed to talk to JJ, I needed to know he was okay. All rational thoughts were out the window as my heart thundered in my chest along with the ringing of my phone in my ear.

"Skye?" JJ answered drowsily.

I tried to answer him. The words got stuck in my throat. I let out a squeak instead. I tried to steady myself enough to talk to him, but I couldn't think. Everything felt rushed and I was starting to shake. It was a full blown attack. I had almost forgotten what they felt like. My skin was crawling, and I felt like I needed to get out of it. My mind started to race with thoughts of everything and nothing all at the same time.

"Do you need me, sweetheart?" I heard him ask, his voice much steadier. I could hear him pulling on jeans and the ruffling a shirt being pulled over his head as he held the phone to his ear.

"Yes," I got out on a breath gripping the phone to my ear as a lifeline.

"On my way," he told me as I heard his truck start. "Can you make it to the door or should I use the key?"

"Key," I whispered rocking forward and back, trying to hold on to what little sanity I felt I had left.

"Okay. I am pulling by the lodge now. Where are your meds, love?"

I closed my eyes and tried to think. Had I even had the prescription filled when I had come home? No, but I had one filled just before I left New York. My brain was still racing and trying to come up with where I had packed them was not working. I heard him pull in and not long after I heard him unlocking the door and coming in. He took the stairs in twos and next thing I knew he was pulling the phone from my hand and putting them both down on the nightstand. He took one look at me and immediately ran downstairs. I heard him get into the refrigerator and seconds later I heard him rummaging around in the bathroom cupboards looking for my Xanax. He found it fairly quickly and was back upstairs shoving the water and a pill into my hands.

"Take it, it will help you calm down and sleep," he told me pushing it back towards me when I shook my head.

I hated the way the pills made me feel, however I hated the feeling of a panic attack more. I popped the pill into my mouth and took a swig of water before curling up on my side in the fetal position. I heard JJ taking off his shirt, boots, and pants before the bed dipped and he pulled my back flush against his chest. He held me lightly, running one hand up and down my arm slowly. The pills started taking effect and everything slowed.

"I love you, JJ," I murmured as I rolled over and snuggled into his chest. I needed to feel him and smell him. I needed to feel safe and he did that for me.

"I love you too, Skye," he responded twining his legs with mine and pressing a kiss to my forehead. "Now sleep, we can talk in the morning."

The last coherent thought I had before the drug induced sleep took over was that I wanted him by my side every night. I was more scared of losing him forever, then I was of the nightmares. He made the panic attacks much

Finding the Way Home
Marcie Shumway

more bearable. I felt strong with him wrapped around me.
I took a deep breath and let the deep sleep take over.

<u>Chapter 16</u>

I woke up the following morning with a cotton mouth and a heavy head, the classic signs of a Xanax hangover. I reached out for JJ only to find a cold bed. I rolled over on my back and listened. I could hear him down in the kitchen rustling around and it was comforting to know he hadn't left. Checking my phone, I gasped at the time. It was well after ten and he should have been at the shop working already. I scrambled to get out of the bed and head downstairs. Before I could even get my feet untangled from the sheets JJ was at the top of the stairs holding a plate with toast and a banana in one hand and a glass of orange juice in the other.

"Good morning sleepyhead," he greeted setting everything down on the nightstand closest to me and leaning down to drop a quick kiss on the top of my head.

"Shouldn't you be at the shop?" I asked settling back down against the pillows and taking in the fact that he had only pulled on his jeans before going down to make me breakfast.

"The shop can run without me for one day," he replied climbing back into bed beside me. "I wanted to make sure you were going to be okay."

I grabbed a piece of toast and quickly started shoving pieces into my mouth. I wasn't sure I was ready to tell him about the nightmare that I had had. The ones with Steve just beating on me were nothing compared to having one about JJ being killed. It made my heart pick up pace just to think about it. As I stared into space contemplating what to tell him and eating my breakfast I felt his hands start to massage my shoulders. I shifted over so that I sat between his legs and let him work his magic. The muscles in my back started to unravel beneath his hands and soon breakfast and the nightmare were long forgotten.

In a daze I reached down and pulled my t-shirt over my head. His hands stalled only long enough for me to remove my shirt and continued working the kinks out of my muscles starting between my shoulder blades and working his way down towards my tail bone. Feeling my core start to warm I put my hands on his thighs and began kneading them, leaning back to press my bare back against his bare chest. JJ's hands came around to cup my breasts, pinching my nipples between his thumbs and fingers, as his mouth came down to place sweet soft kisses on my neck and shoulders. I moaned and pushed myself tighter against him only to find his member hard and pressing into my lower back.

Slowly, so as not to break the sweetness of the moment, I turned and straddled him locking my legs behind his back, pushing my core to his teasingly. His hands came up to pull and push me against him mimicking the sex act. Bringing my hands up to wrap around his neck I found his mouth with mine and sucked his lower lip into my mouth eliciting a low moan from deep inside him. Our kisses were sweet and hot all at the same time, his tongue searching my mouth and mating with mine, caressing gently. Somewhere, somehow we had both stripped off our remaining clothes and before I knew it he was grabbing a condom from the drawer to put on while holding me up with one arm. I continued kissing him and let out a sigh mixed with a purr as he gradually sheathed himself to the hilt within me.

The pace was slow. So different from the first time. It was full of soft murmurs and kisses, sensual touches, and friction so powerful it would give you goosebumps. I had never felt anything like it. As my body started to tighten around him, and his started to harden in response, I locked my blue eyes with his green ones and we watched each other go over the edge. We smiled at each other almost shyly as he maneuvered us so that I was laying beneath him. Pulling out he got up from the bed and made his way downstairs. I heard the water run and soon he was back beside the bed with a warm washcloth in hand. He cleaned me up gently, and after throwing it in the pile of dirty clothes he climbed back into bed to spoon me. Pulling my back flush against his chest and nuzzling into my neck. After a few moments I decided it was time to talk.

"I had a nightmare that Steve had found your house and broke in," I started.

"Skye, you don't need..."

I squeezed his hand that was encased in mine against my belly. It was easier to tell him this way. Both of us warm and calm from lovemaking, and my back to him so that I didn't see his face as I told him.

"All I remember is realizing that we were at your house and I was looking everywhere for you. When I finally could see where you were... you were in a pool of blood," I whispered. Tears I hadn't realized had started were flowing down my cheeks. JJ gripped me tighter and I could hear his breath becoming labored as his anger grew.

"When I noticed you weren't moving I gave up. I was going to let him kill me because without you, life didn't matter. It just wasn't worth living."

"Oh baby," he murmured rolling me over to my other side so I was facing him.

"JJ, I want to be with you so bad and be happy, but I can't seem to let go of this fear that he is going to come here and find me."

"He is never going to hurt you again," he informed me lifting my chin up with is finger so that I could look him in the eyes. "Chad and I wouldn't let anything happen to you. I'm not going anywhere. We will get through all of this together."

I sighed and closed my eyes as his hands started to wander again. He offered comfort in the only way he knew would help me forget and I took it. Riding out the emotions, as I let myself get lost in his touch again.

A few hours later after we had showered and cleaned up from breakfast I was back up in my room looking at empty suitcases and boxes. JJ came up behind me and chuckled as I shook my head.

"You really don't have to do this if you aren't ready."

"I'm ready," I said letting out an exasperated sigh as I started opening drawers and pulling my clothes out.

"But?"

"How does everything feel so right, so quickly with us?" I asked turning to look at him as he placed items from the nightstand into a box.

"I honestly can't tell you," he replied, "but I am not going to question it. I am going to take full advantage of a second chance with you."

I felt my insides turn to mush at that statement and I smiled at him. The wattage in the smile he returned was enough to put my mind at ease. We continued packing and each time that niggling fear would pop up I would look over at him and it would instantly go away. We had always gotten along as kids and then as teenagers. Our friendship was never one we had to work too hard at, it just was. Maybe it was inevitable that he would be my first for so many things and that we were now getting another shot. I saw him stop packing and noticed he was looking at something that he had pulled from one of the drawers. Curious I made my way to him and peaked around his arm to see what he was looking at.

It was a frame that had two pictures in it. On one side was a picture of the six of us that had been taken at our last big party at the lodge before I had left for college, and on the other side was a picture of JJ and I that Sam had taken without us knowing. We had just shared a hug and were pulling away from each other, eyes still connected. She had given me the picture just before I had boarded the plane to New York and it had remained by my side ever since. It had started more than one fight between Steve and I towards the end.

I placed a kiss on JJ's cheek and went downstairs to start packing up my bathroom stuff. Humming away to myself I couldn't contain my smile. JJ was right. We were getting a second chance and there was no reason to question it. I made up my mind then and there that I would go with the flow and just see where this led us. I knew where I wanted it to go, yet I also knew that I needed to get through some things first. Opening the doors under the sink I pulled a few items out that were mine and moved on to the drawers. As I took out Q-tips, hair ties, and make-up I found a half used box of tampons and froze. I hadn't used them since before that first night with JJ. I sat down hard on the toilet cover. Well didn't that throw a whole 'nother wrench into the works.

<u>Chapter 17</u>

I couldn't get that box out of my head the next few days as we moved my things into JJ's place. I didn't say anything to him just yet. I wanted to be sure of what we were dealing with. I racked my brain trying to remember when my last period was, and what the date had been the first night with JJ, the night that we hadn't used any protection. The dates just weren't making sense. I was two weeks late and somehow I hadn't realized it before now.

The next day after I finished a trail ride with some of the campers I went to Haggerty's and grabbed a few groceries and a box of pregnancy tests. I knew I could chalk it up to stress, but I didn't think I was under that much. As I checked out and made my way home I checked in with myself. The idea of being pregnant didn't scare me, surprisingly. Especially not with JJ. I knew he would be a great provider and father. He also loved me, that wasn't even a question. I smiled pulling into the driveway. Everything really would be okay.

My phone vibrated against my hip as I was bringing in the grocery bags. I put away the stuff that needed to be put in the refrigerator and freezer before pulling it out of my pocket. It was Sam.

Girls night? Dinner at The Pit?
Sounds good. What time? Should I grab Morgan?
6:30 :) Already texted her. Pick her up at the lodge?
Of course! Can't wait to see you!

Setting my phone down I looked the clock, 5:30. I only had an hour. I put all my other groceries away with lightning speed. Knowing that if the pregnancy test was positive I wouldn't be able to keep it to myself, I tucked it under the sink in JJ and I's bathroom where he wouldn't look. I wanted to know for sure before I told him, and I wanted him to be the first to know.

Pulling out a pair of jeans and a flowy dress shirt, I took a quick a shower and put on a light coating of make-up. Getting dressed quickly I ran a brush through my hair and pulled on my boots in record time. Grabbing my keys and my cell phone I scribbled a quick note for JJ in case he got back to the house before I did, and I ran out to the truck.

The lodge was lit up like a Christmas Tree when I pulled in and I smiled to myself as kids of various campers could be seen running around and playing in the pool. Parents sat outside talking and enjoying drinks. It was a happy warm sight. I sighed knowing that could be JJ and I someday. It no longer scared me to think of him and I moving forward, getting married, and having a family and a future together. We had done a lot of talking over several days and it had helped dramatically.

"What are you smiling about?" Morgan asked as she climbed into the passenger and shut the door behind her.

"The future," I told her smiling even wider. "Let's go enjoy some time with the girls."

By the time we had pulled up into The Pit we were chatting like teenage girls. It felt so good to be looking forward to time with them and not dreading it. When we got inside Sam and Lisa were already there waiting. They both jumped up, and hugs were had all around before we sat down and ordered a round of appetizers.

Conversation flowed well and there wasn't one time where things were awkward with Lisa. It seemed that JJ was right and that she had changed. She even talked as though she was genuinely happy for JJ and I. As dessert was being placed in front of us my phone vibrated across the table where we had all set our phones. Sam raised her eyebrow as she took a bite of her cheesecake.

"It's probably just JJ," I said laughing.

"Oh, speaking of JJ," Lisa chimed in taking a sip of her wine to wash down the piece of pie she was eating.

Both of Sam's eyebrows came up and she nearly choked on her dessert, as did Morgan. I smiled at them both. Lisa had changed and I wasn't worried about what was about to come out of her mouth.

"Not that way," she waved off their concern taking another bite of her pie. "A gentleman came into the shop this morning asking about you. Said he was a friend of yours from New York and was in town vacationing with his family."

The panic that normally would have set in at that statement didn't. I racked my brain trying to think of who it might be. I hadn't had many close friends while in New York that were just mine. Most of them were people that had been friends of Steve's that I knew through him. Eric and Shelly had been the only ones that had been just mine and I hadn't talked to Shelly since I had left. She had worked at the same firm with Steve, and she had struggled with being my friend and keeping her job. I didn't hold anything against her, I just hadn't had the time to keep up with the friendship, honestly.

"Hmm...wonder who it was. Did he tell you his name?" I asked drinking the last of my water and reaching for my purse to pay the bill the waitress had set down by my elbow.

"Alec? Andrew? It started with an A I think," she responded pulling the bill from my hands so that her and Sam could pay for it for me. "I was in the middle of a shipment so I didn't really talk to him long."

"Huh." I was stumped, but my phone vibrating again interrupted any thoughts I may have had.

"Clearly someone misses you," Sam teased as we all got up to leave and collected our respective phones.

My smile returned and I felt my cheeks get warm. I couldn't remember the last time I had blushed. The girls continued to pick on me as we made our way out to our vehicles. Hugs were exchanged again and we all decided that this was now going to be a weekly thing. It felt so good to have friends again.

After dropping Morgan off at the lodge I made my way back to JJ's, my mind a pile of mush. I couldn't ever recall being happier. As I pulled into the house I remembered that my phone had gone off while we were at dinner. I checked it as I was walking in the front door and found that one was from JJ telling me he loved me and the other was from Eric telling me that he needed to talk to me, so to call him when I had a chance.

I put my purse down on the table by the door and made my way upstairs with my phone in my hand ready to start dialing Eric's number as I walked into our bedroom. All at the same time JJ came out of our bathroom fresh from a shower. His hair was still wet and only a towel covered him, hanging low on his hips. Water droplets glistened on his chest and a sly smile covered his lips. I took him in from head to toe. As he pulled the towel loose

Finding the Way Home
Marcie Shumway

and his member sprang free, hard and ready, I decided
that Eric could definitely wait until the next morning.

<u>Chapter 18</u>

The next morning, I was woken up by my phone vibrating across the night stand. I moaned when I saw what time it was. Seven o'clock and I had the day off. JJ had already left for the shop and I had been looking forward to sleeping in, especially after we had been up most of the night. I rolled over pulling the covers over my head to block the sun with all intents of going back to sleep when I heard my phone go off a second time.

"It had better be good..." I mumbled reaching for my phone and clearing the screen to see who had been texting me. It was Eric. *Call me* and *Now*.

I sighed and reached for JJ's shirt that was thrown on his side of the bed. Pulling it on I made my way out of my cocoon and towards the bathroom. At that moment I remembered the pregnancy test and figured now would be the best time to take it. It would give me time to process the results before I told JJ and no one else was around. I dug around under the sink and found the box. I opened it, read the instructions, and proceeded to do my business. While I was waiting for the two minutes to be up my phone started to vibrate across the vanity. It was Eric calling this time. Without really thinking I answered.

"Hello."

"Do you not answer text messages or read them for that matter?" came the aggravated reply from the other end of the phone.

"I'm sorry," I told him slapping my hand against my forehead, "I have been a bit distracted lately."

"I don't even want to know," he said chuckling lightly. I smiled even though I knew he couldn't see me.

"I need to tell you something and I need you to not freak out."

"Why would I freak out?" I asked pulling my phone away from my ear to check the time, my two minutes was up.

"Steve is MIA and has taken a couple of weeks off from work," Eric told me all in one breath as I picked up the stick I had peed on just minutes ago.

"I'm pregnant," I gasped unintentionally into the phone, tears instantly welling up in my eyes.

"WHAT?!?!?!?!?" he screeched and I heard a chair hit the floor as though he had stood up too fast.

"I wanted to tell JJ first," I groaned closing my eyes and taking a deep breath.

"Honey, I promise I won't tell him I was the first to know. Are you sure?"

"I peed on a stick," I told him opening my eyes again to look at the digital screen, "Clear Blue Easy doesn't lie."

"Is this good or bad?" he asked unsure how he was supposed to react outside of the shock.

"Oh, good! So good!" I smiled, "Well I think anyway. We both want kids and have talked about having them, but not quite yet."

"He loves you, sweetheart," Eric soothed, "I have told you that before. He will be over the moon."

"I hope so," I replied sitting down on top of the toilet seat still gripping the stick in my hand.

Before Eric had a chance to come back with anything I heard the front door open and close and footsteps coming up the stairs two at a time. Seconds later JJ was poking his head into the bathroom door with a concerned look on his face.

"Hey, is everything..." he trailed off having noticed the box on the counter and the stick in my hand.

"Eric... let me call you back. JJ just got home."

"That's fine. Be excited, Skye, you deserve it!"

"Thank you, handsome," I said quietly hanging up, JJ's eyes burning into mine.

"How? When?" JJ stammered, gesturing towards the pregnancy test and box.

"That day that Lisa ticked me off and we forgot the condom," I told him standing up to put the box away, trying to keep my hands busy. "I wondered when we were packing up the cabin, and I realized I hadn't had my period in a while."

He stood staring at me, his mouth dropped open. I wasn't sure how I was supposed to react or what to do. I certainly hadn't expected him to be speechless. I handed him the stick with the cap now firmly in place and he took it looking at the screen. Seconds later his face lit up with a huge smile and his eyes came back up to meet mine.

"We are having a baby," he whispered, reaching his other hand up to cup my cheek.

"We are having a baby," I replied just as quietly, tears flowing freely down my face.

He gathered me in his arms and we cried together in shock and happiness. I'm not sure how long we stood there, but after a while JJ reached around me to start the shower and the two of us undressed each other and climbed in. As I washed his hair JJ put body wash on my loofa and proceeded to wash every part of me, paying special attention to my still flat stomach. There was nothing sexual about it at all. We just enjoyed being with each other and the touching seemed to sooth us both and level the energy back out.

"Are you going to call the doctor?" JJ asked as he toweled dried my hair and I applied moisturizer to my face.

"Yep," I said turning around to apply some cream to his face as well. He wrinkled his nose up at the smell but stood still for my ministrations. I laughed as he pinned me to the counter with his body and rubbed his whiskered chin in the crook of my neck.

"How come you came home?" I asked swatting him away to brush my teeth.

"I couldn't seem to concentrate after last night," he said lathering his face with shaving cream to clean up around his goatee and throwing me a wink.

I rolled my eyes and continued my morning ritual. It felt so good to be standing side by side sharing in these little moments. I smiled at him in the mirror and felt my stomach flip when he flashed me his killer smile in return. My heart swelled. This was the start to something wonderful, and I couldn't wait to see what happened next.

As I spit the last of my toothpaste into the sink, what Eric had said to me on the phone sank in. I was surprised that instant panic didn't set in. Instead I was drawn back to the baby growing inside me, and JJ humming along to the radio in the bedroom as he pulled on clean boxer briefs and Carhartts. Suddenly I wasn't worried about Steve and what he could do to me. I was more concerned about being happy and enjoying this next big thing in my life. I couldn't let him chase me away from happiness forever. I was ready to be free.

Chapter 19

The next morning, I made my way to the office at the lodge and settled in to catch up on some paperwork. That afternoon I was scheduled for a trail ride with Morgan and a group of women campers that were staying in one of the cabins for a week on a girls-only vacation, so I wanted to get all the book work done that I could so I wouldn't be too far behind. A couple of hours in JJ appeared at the door covered in grease and carrying a bag from Doc's Donuts with an iced coffee in his hand. I raised my eyebrow at the coffee and laughed when he turned it to show me it was decaf. I had told him that there were things I would have to change about my diet knowing I was pregnant, and had made sure to ask the doctor's office when I called to schedule my appointment about a few of them. We had our first appointment the following week.

I gave him a thank-you kiss and shooed him out of the office, laughing as he turned to brush his hand across my belly when he was sure there wasn't anyone else around. We had agreed to keep it a secret until we were sure everything was going to be okay with the baby. I went back to entering invoices and preparing those for payment that needed to go out that week. Before I knew it I was backing up my QuickBooks file and was gathering up those that I knew needed Karen or Duncan's approval before I sent them out. Just as I was turning off the computer Duncan stepped into the office.

"There is my other favorite girl!" he exclaimed pulling me in for a bear hug. "Seems like I haven't seen you much lately."

"We had dinner just last week," I reminded him as I sat back down and spread out the invoices for his inspection and signature.

"I know. Just seems weird that you aren't living here and that you are with JJ." he mumbled signing checks one after the other without looking up.

"I thought you had always wanted JJ and I to be together? I thought you loved him like a son?" I asked placing my hand on his to still his actions, causing him to look up at me.

"Oh honey, I do love him and I am so glad you are with him and happy. You deserve it," Duncan told me putting his hand over mine. "I have just been remembering when I was the only man you needed in your life."

"Spoken like a true daddy," I replied tears welling up in my eyes as I leaned over and kissed him on the cheek.

The two of us continued to work side by side until we had all the bills done and ready to be mailed. As we were getting ready to leave the office Chad appeared at the door, his face white and the muscle ticking on his jaw. Duncan looked at him questioningly, but his eyes instantly came to meet mine bypassing his father completely.

"Chad?"

"Skye, you have company."

We followed Chad out to the check-in area and before I could press Chad about who the visitor was I saw him. Steve stood at the counter making what looked to be small talk with Karen. He hadn't changed much in the last eight months. I stopped and took him in. His blonde hair was cut short and neat and he looked every bit the executive he was. He was dressed in a white polo that set off his tan from his weekends in the Hamptons, khakis shorts, leather flip flops, and a gold Rolex on his wrist catching the sun. How had I ever been with him? Looking at him now and comparing him to JJ, who had come into the lodge and now stood behind him still in his greased up Carhartts and white t-shirt from that morning, I don't know how I had ever been with him. I took a deep breath, threw Chad and JJ a reassuring smile and continued forward to stand beside Karen behind the counter.

"Hello, Steve, what can I do for you?" I asked making sure to keep my tone light and happy despite the fact that my knees were literally shaking.

"Skye, wow! You look amazing!" he gushed as he reached for one of my hands with both of his.

"Thank you," I returned allowing him to shake my hand and quickly extracting it before he could kiss the back of it.

"I was hoping we could talk in private," he said dropping his voice a notch so as not to be heard by the campers that were starting to stream in for lunch.

"Did you forget you aren't supposed to be within 100 feet of me?" I asked trying to keep the disbelief from my face and my voice.

"No, I know I'm not supposed to be here, but I really want to apologize and clear the air between us," he stated darting a look to his right as JJ made his way around him and came to stand behind me, putting a hand on my hip.

I struggled with my decision on whether or not to talk to him. He looked genuine and he showed no signs of being bothered by the intimacy of JJ's touch and proximity to my body. I turned and saw the controlled anger in Chad and JJ, and the concern in Karen and Duncan. I needed to close this part of my life and move on. Until I spoke with Steve I wouldn't be able to do that, or feel free from his grip.

"Okay. We can talk, but not alone. JJ, Duncan, and Karen will be there and Chad can take my trail ride this afternoon," I told him turning back around to face him and placing my hand on top of JJ's that had gripped my hip tighter at my words.

Chad's mouth dropped open and he moved to come towards us, however Duncan put his hand on his arm and pointed towards the door. They made eye contact for a moment and unspoken words were passed between them before Chad let out a huff of air and made his way out the door.

"That's fine," Steve finally replied smiling sweetly.

"You can meet us back here in an hour and a half," Duncan told him, "we will be done the lunch rush by then and we won't be disturbed."

"Sounds good."

With that he turned and headed out the door waving as he walked out. I let out the breath I had been holding and leaned back against JJ, soaking up his familiar scent and warmth for strength. The next thing I knew he was guiding me towards the den and Karen and Duncan were heading towards the kitchen together. The minute we were alone in the room I turned into JJ's arms and pulled his mouth down to mine. The kiss was filled with passion, heat, and love. I opened my mouth and drove my tongue into his to circle and tease as I ground my hips against him. He groaned into my mouth and his hands slid down my back to cup my ass and pull me flush. We heard the door click behind us and slowly pulled out of the kiss, breathing heavily with our foreheads still touching.

"Are you okay?" he asked running his fingers down my cheeks.

"More than okay," I told him pulling away enough to see that Karen had put two plates with sandwiches and chips on the small table by the door before she had closed it. "I have you, our baby, and a wonderful family. Once I talk to him I can completely move on."

"Are you sure?"

"Yes," I replied giving him a quick kiss and stepping back to grab the two plates.

We ate lunch silently and I was more than ready when Karen came back in an hour later. She took me into her arms and without saying anything offered me comfort and strength. With the three of them I could do anything. I felt stronger than I had in months and I was ready to face my demons.

A half hour later Duncan came into the room followed by Steve. Seeing him again didn't shake me up as I had expected. I actually didn't feel anything, no remaining love or fear. I was already starting to move forward and to shed the stereotypical signs of a battered woman. I was no longer the victim.

He took a seat on the couch beside Karen since JJ and I had already occupied the loveseat with our thighs touching and my left hand held strongly in his left as he leaned his right across the back. His nonchalant attitude was a complete cover as I could feel the controlled anger radiating off him. Duncan poured the three of the men shots from his favorite decanter and was surprised when JJ nodded his head towards the table for his. He wasn't letting go of me with Steve in the room.

"I want to start by saying that I am so sorry for everything that happened between us," Steve voiced as he took the glass from Duncan and nodded. "I never should have done what I did, and I have been going to counseling regularly since you left."

"Sorry will never be enough," I told him, choosing my words carefully, "I appreciate that you have come all this way, but I can't accept your apology."

JJ squeezed my hand in support and I turned to smile gratefully at him. When I turned back to Steve his mouth hung open in surprise. He closed it and took a quick swallow from his glass. His face looked calm, yet sad. None of the anger I had seen that last night with him was there.

"You turned my life upside down. You took away all my confidence and made me afraid of everyone and everything. It has taken me time to get where I am at now and I still have so much to work on to get back to the person I used to be. So an apology will never be enough."

The room remained quiet. Duncan stood by his minibar with a smile on his face and Karen sat beside Steve looking every bit the proud momma. JJ leaned in and kissed my temple and I gripped his hand firmly. Steve slowly started to stand and when I looked up at him he had tears in his eyes, and a few had escaped down his cheeks.

"I truly am sorry for everything, Skye," he whispered loud enough for me to hear as I stood up. He made his way past us towards the door. "I hope you are happy and that he treats you a whole hell of a lot better than I did."

With those final words he walked out the door and Duncan followed, I am sure to confirm that he actually left. Karen stood and came to me again hugging me and offering me her love without a single word. She kissed my forehead and made her way to follow Duncan and Steve out. JJ turned me into his arms and I gripped his torso tightly as I laid my head against his chest with a deep sigh. His hands made comforting circles on by back and I closed my eyes as I felt his breath against my face.

"I'm so proud of you, baby," he murmured, "You have come so far in such a short amount of time. I am so lucky to have a woman like you in my life, having my baby. I love you so much."

"I couldn't have done it without you," I told him pulling back to look into his eyes and smile lovingly at him. "Coming home was the best thing I could have done for myself. I am so lucky to have found a man like you that I can lean on and have my baby with. I love you too."

<u>Chapter 20</u>

The week following our meeting with Steve seemed to go by in a blur. I got back into my routine at the lodge even with some slight morning sickness and extreme exhaustion. Despite everything I felt great and after everything with Steve I felt like a weight had been lifted. Both Chad and JJ hovered at my every move making sure I wasn't ever left alone and that I was handling it all okay. No matter how much I told them that I was fine after he had left that day, they didn't seem to believe me.

JJ and I snuck to our first doctor's appointment, somehow, without anyone knowing and had found out that I was already 9 weeks along. We decided that even though the ultrasound looked good and the doctor assured us all was progressing nicely we would wait until I was 12 weeks along before telling anyone. We wanted to make sure I was into the "safe zone", plus come up with a cute and creative way to tell them.

Two days following the doctor's appointment I had a particularly rough bout of morning sickness. I locked myself in the bathroom, not wanting JJ to see me as I got sick, and hugged the toilet for all I was worth. Clearly I hadn't gotten up early enough to eat something, which calmed my stomach as I had been doing every other morning. Instead I had rolled over hoping for the extra ten minutes as JJ was getting breakfast ready downstairs. The baby had decided it didn't like that idea.

I was finally able to leave the bathroom and when I did JJ was sitting on the side of the bed putting his boots on. He had brought up a banana, dry toast, and ginger ale and they sat on my side of the bed. I crawled up the bed behind him and curled myself around his back. He rubbed my back and pushed my hair away from my face.

"Why don't you go in late this morning? Do they need you first thing?"

"I just texted Karen and told her I thought I had the stomach bug Lisa had last week."

"Only a few more weeks and we can tell them," he assured me standing up and pulling the covers back up and over me.

"Please tell me you aren't going to sit here and baby-sit me?"

"No, unfortunately I have a shipment coming in within the next half hour and both Lisa and Will are coming in late. Call me if you need anything at all."

"I'm good. Going to eat, sleep, shower and head to work. I will stop by the shop on my way in," I told him as I tugged the blankets tighter around me and munched on the dry toast.

He kissed my forehead and trudged downstairs. I heard the door click behind him as I finished my first piece of toast. It felt so good to finally have some peace and quiet. As much as I loved JJ, Chad, and the rest of the family, their recent hovering after our meeting with Steve had become a bit overbearing. I polished off the second piece of toast and took a sip of ginger ale. My stomach seemed to have calmed down so I curled up on my side and dozed off.

I'm not sure what woke me up, but a couple hours later I came to. Feeling much better than I had earlier, I grabbed the banana and climbed out of bed. While eating it I scrounged around for clothes for the day and made my way to the bathroom to get ready.

I was scheduled for barn work and a trail ride so a shower wasn't necessary. I pulled on jeans and a flowy tank top. While I was brushing my hair I thought I heard something from downstairs. I stopped moving for a minute to listen, but when I didn't hear anything I went back to French braiding my hair.

Leaving the bathroom, I grabbed my cell phone and socks and headed for the stairs. At the top I heard someone walking around in the living room. Thinking it was JJ, I hopped the rest of the way down and was brought to a dead stop with who I found leaning against the door jam.

Steve stood between me and the door leading outside. He must have been what I heard while getting ready. There was no way that JJ knew he was here because he wouldn't have gotten past the front door.

"Steve, what are you doing here?" I asked more surprised than scared.

"You really thought I was going to let you go that easily?" he sneered. "You really thought I would let that redneck have you?"

I took a step towards the kitchen, knowing that if I could get there even a few steps ahead of him I could get out the sliding glass door and at least scream. He matched my shift with one of his own and a smile. I stopped and stood facing him. I wasn't afraid of him anymore, but I knew I needed to protect my baby if nothing else.

"Huh, so much for you changing," I snorted.

Laughing at him was my first mistake. He didn't take long to swing his arm around to backhand me. I ducked only allowing him a glancing blow that knocked me off balance, yet didn't take me down. I thanked god for the self-defense classes Eric had recommended. While he was still in swing I kicked him in the knee hoping to inflict enough damage to get away. He went down on his good knee gripping the other with one of his hands.

"Bitch!" he howled.

I scrambled towards the kitchen leaning towards the wall in the hallway to try to regain my balance. I didn't get far before I felt his hand clasp around my ankle pulling me down. Before I hit the floor I rolled sideways so that I landed on my side, and not on my belly. I felt a pain go up my arm from the impact. I ignored it and wound up to kick out with the leg he hadn't grabbed.

I felt his nose crunch under my foot as it connected with this face. The satisfaction was short lived as I remembered I hadn't put shoes on and the ball of my foot thudded dully with pain after the collision. It was enough to have him reaching for his nose, unfortunately not with the hand that still held my ankle. I shook the leg he held onto and wound back with my free leg to kick out at him again.

"Obviously they taught you some bad habits we need to get rid of," Steve mumbled grabbing my other foot with the hand that had been holding his nose seconds before.

"They didn't teach me anything," I muttered back struggling against his strength. "I just figured out that you weren't worth the hassle."

He seemed surprised that I even had a comeback and I took advantage of his surprise by wiggling a foot free and quickly smashing him in the face again. I felt his release and didn't look back before pushing to my feet and reaching out to unlock and open the sliding door. Suddenly I was dragged back by my hair and flung towards the island in the middle of the kitchen. I maneuvered myself again so I took as much of the blow to my side as I could. Before I could try to make my way back towards the hallway, he grabbed me and backhanded me again.

My jaw rattled with the force and my eyes watered bringing me to my knees. He brought me back up to a standing position his hand around my neck and my chin resting between his thumb and pointer finger. He pushed me so that my back was against the wall and I felt his fingers start to squeeze. I pulled at him with both hands to distract him from what my feet were doing. Playing the classic panicked woman.

I knew I would only have one shot so I had to make it count. Using my good leg, I picked my knee up with all I had and drove it into his crotch. He let go of my neck quickly and doubled over in pain. I struggled to catch my breath and while I was doing so I heard the front door open and JJ call my name.

"IN HERE!" I yelled as best my voice would allow.

JJ and Chad appeared in the doorway and I heard sirens in the distance. Chad immediately went to Steve and JJ came rushing to me. I collapsed into his arms and put my hands to my stomach. There was pain in my arm and both feet, but everything with the baby felt fine. One of JJ's hands covered mine and he looked at me with concern in his eyes. I shook my head and smiled telling him everything was okay.

He held me tightly until the paramedics and police told him he had to let go long enough to check me out.

Steve had a quick check out, and was escorted out of the house wearing handcuffs, all the while yelling that he wanted a restraining order against me and that I had started all the violence and he had only come to talk to me.

I shook my head as they wheeled me out of the house. Due to the early term of the pregnancy the paramedics had recommended that I go to the hospital to be checked out and JJ had readily agreed. Chad's mouth dropped open at the news. I was bummed he had heard it that way but I smiled and blew him a kiss as I was going past him. He smiled quickly in return and returned my kiss. He and JJ hugged before JJ climbed into the back of the ambulance with me.

As we pulled out of the driveway I let out a big breath. It was finally all over. Steve would be out of our lives for good and I was going to have a baby with the man of my dreams. I closed my eyes and let the hum of the ride and the feeling of JJ's hands rubbing mine relax me. The other shoe had dropped and I had come out on the other side stronger than I had started.

<u>Chapter 21</u>

Almost three months later, I breathed out a sigh of relief as the sun topped the trees and the sky remained completely blue without a cloud in sight. It was going to be a beautiful fall day and I couldn't be more appreciative of that. Today I was marrying JJ.

My hands went to my belly as I gazed out the bedroom window towards the woods. I heard a camera clicking away to my right. At the party at JJ's after Morgan's graduation I had found out Jess Wing was a photographer and she had jumped at the chance to do our pictures. She said that we would never know she was there, and other than the light sounds of the camera, I hadn't.

JJ and I had decided to get married with only our immediate family and friends present in a special clearing in the woods followed by a reception at the lodge with the remaining guests from the camp. I looked down at my growing bump and smiled when I felt a slight kick. We had had our doctor's appointment to find out what we were having a few days prior and we had given the envelope directly to the baker without opening it so we could share it at the reception with everyone. We were both very excited.

"How are you doing in here?" Karen asked poking her head into my bedroom bringing me back from my daydream.

"Great," I told her turning around to face her.

"Baby okay?" she asked putting a hand on top of mine on my belly.

"Yep, I was just thinking and my hands seem to go there on their own."

"That they do," she chuckled giving it a rub and turning to look at my dress hanging from the closet door.

"Isn't it beautiful?" I asked walking over to run my hands down the length of it.

"It is. She would be so happy that you are wearing it."

The dress had been my mother's, well, most of it anyway. Due to my growing midsection we had some alterations done so it would be free flowing, and we updated it to make it a little more modern. I looked over at my bureau where a picture of my mother and I sat that had been taken months before she had died. I knew she was watching over me and her grandchild. Tears started to well up in my eyes.

"None of that!!!" Morgan's hollering jumped me from my thoughts.

I laughed and turned to see her, Lisa, and Sam in the doorway. All three wore burgundy ankle length dresses with V-necks and wide straps. Simple heels adorned all their feet, and necklaces that JJ and I had bought them completed the ensemble. They all looked beautiful. Again I felt the tears.

"Stop it!" Morgan said again handing me a tissue, "You will ruin your makeup and I spent hours on it!"

The girls quickly bustled around and helped me get into my dress. I watched in the full length mirror as they worked around me touching up my makeup and hair, putting on my earrings, clasping my necklace, and straightening my dress. At that moment I couldn't have felt more loved.

Once I was ready we made our way downstairs to meet up with Duncan. He helped us all load up into the side-by-side and we made our way to a spot just before the clearing to unload. My stomach started to flip flop as the music started and the girls filed towards the clearing ahead of me.

"You ready?" Duncan whispered as I took his arm and fluffed my dress out behind me.

"No and yes, all at the same time," I told him squeezing his arm gently.

When we reached the opening of the clearing all my nervousness evaporated. My eyes found JJ's and no one else existed. The ceremony passed in a blur. The next thing I knew the I dos were said, our rings were exchanged, and we were being presented as Mr. and Mrs. Jonathan Jackson Hunter. The kiss was long and deep enough to have everyone whistling and hooting and hollering. I pulled away blushing slightly as I hooked my arm through his and he led me back down the aisle.

When we reached the reception food was just being set out. JJ and I, along with Chad, Lisa, Sam, Kyle, Morgan, and Eric filed into line first and once we had our plates full we went back to our table. Conversation flowed and laughter blanketed the room. At one point I stopped eating and just took it all in. JJ squeezed my hand drawing my attention to him and he pointed at our wedding cake. I smiled and kissed him. That was how we were going to reveal the gender of our baby. Inside the frosted white cake was a filling colored either pink or blue. We didn't even know what color it was.

Once we were finished eating we made our way around the room hand in hand greeting everyone and talking to them. At one point I heard a giggle to my right and when I turned I noticed Chad and Lisa deep in flirtatious conversation, with her hand on his arm. Huh, that was a new development.

Finally, it was time to cut the cake. The DJ called us over to the cake and prepped the song we had asked him to play. "Twinkle, Twinkle, Little Star" filled the speakers and everyone laughed. With JJ's hand steading mine, we cut into the cake on the backside where only we could see at first. As we slid the piece out I gasped and looked up at JJ. He was grinning ear to ear and his eyes were sparkling. The filling was blue. We were having a boy. Eric Riley Hunter. Taking the piece we had pulled out I fed it to JJ making sure to rub the frosting all over so that everyone could see what color it was. Cheers erupted as we shared a kiss and celebrated our news.

We finished with the cake and got ready to dance our first dance as husband and wife. The beginning notes of "I Could Not Ask for More" by Sarah Evans started to play and JJ gathered me in his arms. I sighed in contentment and let him lead the way around the small dance floor.

"Are you happy?" he asked pulling back just enough to look me in the eye.

"Overflowing," I responded running one hand over the soft hair on his neck while the other rested on his chest intertwined with his.

He pulled our joined hands to his lips and kissed my palm. I smiled and closed my eyes. Life couldn't get any better. Wonderful husband, soon-to-be new baby, and the

123

Finding the Way Home
Marcie Shumway

best friends and family a woman could ask for. Who would have known finding the way home after so long would have been this good?

Finding the Way Home
Marcie Shumway